"I hate to tell y_____. But look where Cami's sitting."

Joni glanced around to where Crystal nodded and drew her breath in sharply.

"She's sitting with Todd!" Joni said angrily. "With Todd and Twister and Parker and Jason…and *Beau*!"

Joni's blood started to boil as she watched Cami give Beau a big smile and say something to him. Beau looked self-conscious, but he shrugged and smiled back. Cami turned her attention to Jason, who seemed really pleased, and then back to Beau again.

"Wow! Cami sure isn't shy any more," Su-Su said sarcastically.

Crystal nodded. "You can say that again. Look, she's making up to Twister, of all people! And she's batting her eyes!"

"It's disgusting," said Su-Su. "Look at that! She's got all five boys practically eating out of her hand."

"That little flirt," Joni muttered. "She'd better not think she can make a habit of stealing other girls' boyfriends. And she'd *better* not think she can steal Beau!"

#4
DOUBLE DUMPED

by Betsy Haynes

BULLSEYE BOOKS

Random House   New York

For my terrific friend
Virginia Kinner

A BULLSEYE BOOK PUBLISHED BY RANDOM HOUSE, INC.

Copyright © 1995 by Betsy Haynes.
Cover art copyright © 1995 by Aleta Jenks.

Library of Congress Catalog Card Number: 95-70325
ISBN: 0-679-86025-8
RL: 5.0

Manufactured in the United States of America   10 9 8 7 6 5 4 3 2 1

BOY TALK is a trademark of Random House, Inc., and Betsy Haynes

Chapter One

"Joni! Wait up!"

Joni Sparkman's heart jumped, and she shot a quick glance over her shoulder. She would know that voice *anywhere*.

Beau Maguire was darting and weaving toward her through the crowd of students that was moving slowly through the halls of Sunshine Beach Middle School on the way to last-period class.

"Hey, listen, Joni, I need to talk to you. It's important," he said when he caught up with her.

A rush of happiness swept through her. Beau looked so cute walking beside her, a shock of blond hair falling over his forehead. And she couldn't remember when his eyes had looked so blue.

"What's up?" she asked, grinning at him. Sometimes she had a hard time believing that Beau Maguire, the most popular boy in the entire seventh grade, was *her* boyfriend.

"Don't get mad, 'kay?" he said. "It's just that… well…"

Joni's good mood was gone in a flash. She stopped in the middle of the hall, letting the crowd push past her. "Don't get mad about what?" she asked slowly. She definitely had a bad feeling about this.

Beau stopped, too, looking sheepish. "I can't come over tonight."

Joni stared at him. A moment ago she had been feeling like the luckiest girl alive. She had the two best friends on earth, Su-Su (short for Susan Suzanna) McCarthy and Crystal Britton. And Boy Talk, the romance hot line the three of them had set up in secret on Crystal's father's answering machine, was a blast and a total success. But the greatest thing of all was how well she and Beau had been getting along for the past couple of weeks. They'd had a lot of problems before, but lately he had been spending more time with her than with his obnoxious friends.

Now a sick feeling was forming in the pit of her stomach. Was it his friends again, wrecking things just when everything was going great?

"But we have to study for our big science test," she

reminded him. "It's this Friday, and today's Tuesday. What could be more important than that?"

Beau glanced away, looking even more sheepish. "I know we've got the test on Friday, but the guys and I already signed up for the basketball tournament at the Y. It starts tonight. I forgot all about it when I said I'd come over to study."

Joni gritted her teeth. His friends again! Dan Turpin—otherwise known as Twister—Jason Duffy, and Parker Hatch were always trying to come between the two of them. Sometimes it made her so furious she could hardly stand it.

"Well, *fine!*" she exploded. "Go play your basketball at the stupid Y with your stupid friends! See if I care! It's *only* the biggest science test of the year." Whirling away, she took off at a run, dodging the few stragglers left in the hall.

Just as she ducked into the empty girls' rest room, she heard Beau yell after her, "Give me a break, Joni! I've got a life, too, you know!"

She dropped her books on the floor, leaned against the sink, and burst into tears. She knew she shouldn't have let her emotions get the best of her, but sometimes she just couldn't help it.

After a while she glanced up at the face in the mirror and gasped. She hardly recognized herself: the red nose, the puffy eyes, the tear-streaked cheeks. Even her short, dark hair looked like a rat's nest.

"I can't go to class like this!" she whispered in horror.

Class! She'd forgotten all about class. Her eyes dropped to her watch. History had started ten minutes ago. She'd been crying so hard, she hadn't even heard the bell.

"Now what?" she muttered miserably. "If I go in now, how will I explain where I've been and why I look like such a wreck? 'Gosh, Mr. Murphy, I've been in the girls' bathroom crying my eyes out because my boyfriend would rather spend time with his lousy friends than be with me tonight.'"

She sighed and pulled a handful of paper towels from the dispenser on the wall. Wetting them, she pressed the cool towels against her face and tried to decide what to do.

There were forty minutes left until school let out for the day. Joni knew she would probably be safe in the rest room until the dismissal bell. By then her face would be back to normal.

If someone comes in, I'll just tell her I barfed up my lunch, she thought. In fact, that was the excuse she could use tomorrow when she went back to history class.

She grinned at herself in the mirror. She felt just as clever as Lindsey Jones, the heroine of the mystery books she devoured at the rate of two or three a week. Joni planned to write mysteries herself someday. She felt especially proud of herself every time she was able to think like her favorite detective.

In fact, Boy Talk had been Joni's idea. She and Beau had been having major fights, but at that time most of them had been about Beau's habit of putting her down in front of his friends. She had been desperate for advice.

Then one night while she and Su-Su had been over at Crystal's house, they'd seen an ad for a telephone hot line called Romance Rap in a teen magazine. They'd called the number and run up a phone bill of seventy-two dollars and fifteen cents. But unfortunately for Joni, she hadn't gotten the advice she needed.

Then an idea came to her in a flash of serious brilliance. Crystal's father had an answering machine with a separate, unlisted telephone number and was always away in the afternoons, teaching college. Joni, Su-Su, and Crystal could start their own romance hot line on Mr. Britton's answering machine for one hour every day after school, and he would never find out about it. That way they could not only get advice for their own problems but could give advice, too. They could listen in on the problems of girls all over town without anyone knowing it was them. And best of all, it wouldn't cost a cent.

The next day they had secretly circulated a flyer

around school and listened to the buzz grow as every-one started talking about their plans to call in. Joni had a copy of the flyer hidden in her desk drawer at home:

♡ ♡ ♡ ♡ ♡ ♡ ♡ ♡ ♡ ♡ ♡ ♡ ♡ ♡ ♡ ♡ ♡

BOY TALK

♡ *Totally confidential! Absolutely free!*
♡ *Romance! Dating! Friendship!*
♡ *Share your secrets with other teens!*
♡ *Ask for help with your boyfriend problems!*
♡ *Give advice and be a best friend to someone else!*

CALL 555-3902

After school Monday–Friday, 3:30–4:30

♡ ♡ ♡ ♡ ♡ ♡ ♡ ♡ ♡ ♡ ♡ ♡ ♡ ♡ ♡ ♡ ♡

The rest was glorious, beautiful history. She and Beau had resolved their problems with the help of Boy Talk. Crystal had taken two callers' advice and figured out how to convince Evan Byrnes that she could be more to him than just a good friend and the girl next door. Su-Su had volunteered to help out a girl calling herself Too Many Guys, and now Chris Oberlin was her boyfriend.

When the dismissal bell rang, Joni gave her face a final dab with the cool paper towels. Then she headed down the hall to find her friends. It was time to go to Crystal's house and set up the answering machine for today's session of Boy Talk.

Joni could hardly wait. She needed Boy Talk's help in dealing with Beau—*again*.

Chapter Two

"You and Beau had another fight, didn't you?" asked Crystal the moment Joni walked out the front door of the school. Crystal and Su-Su were waiting for her on the top step.

"How can you tell?" Joni asked in surprise. She'd been sure that her eyes weren't red anymore and that her face had lost its puffiness.

Crystal shrugged. "You just have a certain look when you're mad at Beau about something. Is everything okay?"

"To answer your questions, yes, we had another fight, and no, everything isn't okay," Joni admitted.

She could never fool Crystal. Her petite friend, who had honey-blond hair and a dimple that appeared in her left cheek whenever she smiled, was one of the smallest girls in their seventh grade class, but her heart was humongous. Sometimes it seemed as if Crystal had ESP, the way she could sense when something was wrong. And she always knew exactly what to say to make one of her friends feel better.

"He was supposed to come over tonight and study for our big science test on Friday, but he's going to play basketball at the Y with his friends instead," said Joni.

"Pond scum," muttered Su-Su. She tossed her long, wavy red hair over her shoulder. "He doesn't deserve a girlfriend like you, Joni. Seriously, did you ever consider that he may have been switched at birth with a subhuman life form?"

Joni couldn't help smiling. Su-Su had her own bizarre way of brightening things up.

"You might be right," she said. "But we'd better get to Crystal's if we're going to get Boy Talk started on time."

Half an hour later, Joni, Crystal, and Su-Su were sitting around the desk in Mr. Britton's office, waiting for the first call of the day to come in.

It wasn't long before the phone rang and the recorded Boy Talk greeting came on the answering machine. Su-Su loved being dramatic, so she had done the voice in a fake English accent to hide her identity.

"Hello, welcome to Boy Talk. Thank you ever so

much for ringing up." Then the voice explained how to leave a message after the beep or punch 1 to listen to the messages that had already been recorded that day.

Beep.

"Great, our first call," said Joni eagerly. Somehow, listening to Boy Talk helped her forget about her own problems for a while.

"Hi, Boy Talk. This is Lip Service," a girl said in a disgusted voice. "I went out with this really cute boy, and he wanted to kiss me. I just wasn't ready, so I said no. The next day my friend told me he was spreading it around school that he would never ask me out again. I asked him why, and he said it was because I wouldn't kiss him." She paused. "Now he won't even talk to me. What should I do?"

"More pond scum," said Su-Su. "Boys can be such jerks sometimes."

"She probably hurt his feelings," Crystal said sympathetically. "Who knows? It might have taken him ages to get up his nerve to try to kiss her, and she shot him down."

"Maybe it was the way she shot him down that made him mad," Joni suggested. "Maybe instead of explaining how she felt about kissing, she gave him the impression that the problem was him."

The jangle of the phone put an end to the discussion.

Beep.

"Hi, Boy Talk. I've got a big problem with my boyfriend. He's been acting really cold to me lately. He acts like he likes just about everybody else better than me, even my best friend. But when I told him how I felt, he got mad. He said I was just jealous over nothing. I'm not convinced. How can I tell if he wants to break up with me? Suspicious is my first, middle, and last name!"

"Wow, is she ever steamed," said Su-Su.

"Hey, guys," Joni said, frowning. "Didn't that voice sound familiar to you?"

"Not particularly," said Crystal.

Su-Su shook her head. "Me, either."

"It sounded like Marissa Pauley to me," said Joni. "Her locker is next to mine. I talk to her practically every day."

"Come to think of it, that did sound like Marissa," said Su-Su. "Doesn't she go out with Todd Merrill?"

"Right," said Crystal. "Todd took her to the Beach Bash, and they've been dating ever since. If it really was Marissa, it sounds as if they may be breaking up."

The phone rang three more times, but no one left any messages. That meant the callers were probably listening to messages. Joni figured it wouldn't be long before advice started pouring in.

She was right. The next caller had plenty to say.

Beep.

"Boy Talk, this is a call for Suspicious from Understands the Problem. Believe me, there are lots of things to watch for if you think your boyfriend wants to break up. One sign is that, every time you call him, he says he can't talk because someone else needs to use the phone. Another sign is when he calls a date off at the last minute and makes a lame excuse. But the worst for me was when he left his seat in the movie to get popcorn and came back empty-handed. I know it was because he went to talk to some other girl. He said he forgot, and that if I really wanted some popcorn, he'd go back and get it."

Beep.

"Hi, Boy Talk. I've got a message for Suspicious. Watch out when his friends act kind of weird and embarrassed whenever you bring up his name. They probably know something you don't. And watch out when he doesn't want to spend much money on you anymore. He's probably spending it on somebody else. I know what I'm talking about. Call me Cheated On."

Beep.

"Boy Talk? This is for Suspicious. When my boyfriend wanted to break up with me, he started being really critical of everything I said or did. He suddenly didn't like my clothes or the way I wore my hair. Then he started saying he needed space, when we were barely even seeing each other anymore. The next thing I knew, we broke up and he started going with someone else. You can call me Brokenhearted, because that's what I am."

The phone was silent after Brokenhearted hung up.

Joni thought about Suspicious and all the girls who had called to tell her what to look for. "I guess I'm pretty lucky with Beau, after all," she said. "My only competition these days is basketball and Twister, Parker, and Jason."

Before Su-Su or Crystal could reply, the phone rang.

Beep.

"I really need your help, Boy Talk, and there's no one else I can talk to," a girl's voice said just above a whisper. "I have a killer crush on a boy who... whoops, I can't tell you that."

She paused, and Joni, Su-Su, and Crystal exchanged puzzled glances.

"Anyway," she went on nervously, "I can't eat. I can't sleep. I can't do anything but dream about him. He likes me, too, but we can't be seen together. I can't explain why. Trust me. Something *awful* would happen. But I'm *so* miserable. What can I do?"

There was another silence. "Just call me His Secret Love," she added shyly and hung up.

Joni jumped out of her chair the instant the tape shut off. This time she was positive she knew who the caller was. "That was Cami Petre! I'm sure it was," she said excitedly.

"Do you mean the Cami Petre who just happens to be Marissa Pauley's best friend?" asked Su-Su.

"The same person Marissa's boyfriend fixed up with Marc Howe for the Beach Bash so they could double?" Crystal asked in amazement.

Joni nodded. "You've got it," she said slowly. She looked from one of her friends to the other. "There's definitely something funny going on here."

Chapter Three

The next two calls that came in were for Lip Service. One suggested that Lip Service have another talk with the boy and tell him not to take it personally that she refused to kiss him. The other told her to forget the boy. If he put too much pressure on her for a kiss, the caller pointed out, just think what he might do later.

Joni only half listened to the calls. Her mind was on Marissa and Cami. She knew they had been best friends for a long time. It would be awful if their friendship broke up over Todd Merrill.

"Guys," Joni said when the second caller hung up, "we've got to do something about Marissa and Cami."

"Get serious," said Su-Su. "We aren't even totally

positive they're the ones involved."

"Even if we were, what could we do?" Crystal asked glumly. "Tell Marissa her best friend is trying to steal her boyfriend? Tell Cami to knock it off? Get real."

"That may not be what's going on, anyway," said Su-Su. "I mean, that is what it sounds like, but ..." She shrugged as her voice trailed off.

Joni's thoughts were racing. The trouble with Crystal and Su-Su was that they didn't know how to think like detectives. An idea was starting to form in her mind.

"What if we put messages on Boy Talk for each of them?" she said. "Something that would head off disaster, at least for now. Then we could snoop around at school tomorrow and find out for sure what's going on."

A worried look crossed Su-Su's face. "What kind of messages?"

Joni bit her lower lip and thought a moment. "Well, we could tell Suspicious that she probably has nothing to worry about. We could try to convince her that boys act that way all the time, and it usually doesn't mean anything. Then we could tell His Secret Love that she'd better keep it a secret."

"Joni! That's *awful* advice," scolded Crystal. "That won't help either of them. It'll only make things worse!"

"Only temporarily," Joni insisted. "Just until we find out if we're right about it's being Marissa and Cami. If it is, we can call in to Boy Talk again tomorrow and give them *good* advice."

"You know, your plan is just weird enough that it might work," said Su-Su. "I could record the messages in one of my bogus voices." She tapped a long purple fingernail on the desk and lapsed into thought.

"Okay, everybody," said Joni. "Let's think up some killer messages. Ones that will really do the job."

Suddenly the phone rang again.

Beep.

"Suspicious, are you listening? I know all about boyfriends who cheat. You know why? I just stole mine from somebody else! Is there another girl he pays lots of attention to? Does he laugh at her jokes and just shrug at yours? Does he freak if you say something the tiniest bit negative about her? Is everything *she* does right, and everything *you* do wrong? If you answered yes to any of the above, look out! Your boyfriend is about to be snatched. Call me Thief of Hearts!"

Joni listened in horror to the girl laugh as she hung up. "That does it!" she cried. "We don't have a minute to lose. If Marissa hears that, she'll put two and two together and come up with Cami!"

"I've got an idea," said Crystal. "Why don't we

shut Boy Talk down early, before Suspicious can call in and hear Thief of Hearts's message? Then tomorrow we can put good advice on the tape if we find out it's Marissa and Cami."

Before Joni could say she liked Crystal's idea, the phone rang again.

Beep.

The three girls listened expectantly to the answering machine, but no one said a word onto the tape.

"Uh-oh, someone just called in to listen," said Su-Su. Crystal gasped. "What if it's Suspicious?"

"Well, there's no way to find out," Joni said, "so we can't take any chances. We *have* to put our own messages on now."

Five minutes later, Su-Su picked up the phone in Crystal's bedroom and punched in the Boy Talk number. She held the receiver away from her so that Joni and Crystal could hear the greeting.

"Hello, welcome to Boy Talk. Thank you ever so much for ringing up."

Su-Su put a hand over the mouthpiece. "This is going to be weird. It's like I'm talking to myself," she told Joni and Crystal.

Beep.

"Heeeey, Boy Talk! This is Whoopi Goldberg comin' atcha. I've got a message for Suspicious. Lighten up, sister! You're gonna chase that man of yours into the next county if you keep on hasslin' him like that. So he's a little moody sometimes. So what? You're whatcha call overpossessive, and you're settin' yourself up for grief. Come on, Suspicious. Re-*laaaax!*"

"Su-Su, that was great!" Crystal cried the instant Su-Su hung up. "You sounded exactly like her."

"Wait till you hear this next one," said Su-Su, grinning slyly. "I'm going to ring up now," she added in her fake English accent.

Beep.

"Hello, Boy Talk. This is Lisa Simpson," Su-Su said in a high-pitched nasal twang. "Bart and I heard your message, His Secret Love, and we think you're the coolest! Our advice to you is: *Keep on sneaking!* And one more thing: *Don't get caught!* Hee, hee, hee."

Joni wiped tears of laughter from her eyes as Su-Su hung up and put an arm around her friend. "You may be a little bizarre sometimes, but you're also a genius," she said, shaking her head in wonder. "No one would ever guess that was you."

"But do you think the messages will work?" asked Crystal anxiously.

Joni felt her optimism fade away. "I sure hope so," she murmured.

Chapter Four

Joni had a hard time studying for her science test that night. It wasn't just because Beau wasn't there, either. Her thoughts kept coming back to Marissa Pauley and Cami Petre. She was remembering some things now that hadn't seemed important to her before.

Cami was terribly shy. Sometimes it seemed as if the poor girl followed the outgoing Marissa around like a slave, imitating everything Marissa did. Marissa had straight blond hair. Cami had straight dark hair. Marissa cut her bangs short. Cami cut her bangs short. Then Marissa let her bangs grow out. So did Cami. Cami probably would have exchanged her huge brown eyes for smaller blue ones like Marissa's if she could have. Marissa had had a crush on Todd

"Who knows?" Marissa said finally, shrugging. "If you want to know the truth, I could care less."

Joni's pulse quickened. Marissa was definitely feeling down about something. The trick was going to be to change the subject from the science test to Todd Merrill. Then she had a brilliant idea.

"I know what you mean," said Joni. "Beau was supposed to come over last night to study with me, but he didn't. He decided to play in a stupid basketball tournament at the Y instead. Can you believe that? I tried to study myself, but I was so mad at him that I couldn't get into it."

Marissa looked surprised. "You mean there actually was a basketball tournament at the Y?" she asked. "I thought Todd was just making that up." Then, looking embarrassed, she added, "What I mean is, he hates science, and I thought he was just saying there was a tournament to get out of studying."

Right, thought Joni. *What you really thought was that he was studying with someone else.*

"Guys," Joni said, shaking her head sympathetically. "They're so immature sometimes."

Marissa started to say something else, but just then Beau came rushing up the hall. He screeched to a stop in front of Joni's locker.

"You should have seen me last night, Joni" he began breathlessly. "I was awesome! I scored twenty-four points! Move over, Shaq, here comes Beau Maguire!"

Joni managed a weak smile. "That's great," she said.

If Beau noticed her lack of enthusiasm, he didn't show it. "Man, I was unstoppable," he said. He dribbled an invisible ball in little circles, crouched, and made a jump shot toward an invisible basket, almost landing on Joni's foot. "I was everywhere. Under the basket. In the other guy's face. It was so cool!" He grinned proudly and raked a lock of blond hair off his forehead.

"What about Todd?" Marissa asked eagerly. "Were you guys on the same team?"

Beau had started dribbling again, but now he stopped. "Todd?" he asked, frowning at Marissa. "You mean Todd Merrill?"

"Of course," said Marissa.

"Nah, he wasn't on my team," said Beau. "In fact, I don't remember him being there at all."

Marissa stared at Beau, and the smile faded from her face. "Oh," she said, barely above a whisper.

Joni watched the blond girl turn slowly and walk down the hall, without even closing her locker. Joni quickly closed Marissa's locker and her own. Then Joni headed toward class, Beau still happily dribbling alongside her.

"So what's the matter with Marissa?" asked Beau, taking another fake shot.

"I have no idea," Joni mumbled, but deep down she *did* know.

There was no more doubt. Marissa really *was* Suspicious, and her boyfriend had probably spent the evening with His Secret Love.

Chapter Five

"Now all we have to do is find out if Cami is His Secret Love," Joni said when she met Crystal and Su-Su in the cafeteria at noon. She had just finished telling her friends about the scene with Marissa and Beau at her locker that morning.

"How are we going to do that?" asked Crystal. "We can't exactly walk up to Cami and ask her."

"I wish I knew what zodiac signs Marissa and Cami and Todd were born under," said Su-Su. "Their horoscopes would give us a lot of clues."

"Get serious, Su-Su," said Joni, giving her an exasperated look. "What we need is a *real* solution, not a lot of hocus-pocus."

Su-Su sat up straighter and raised her eyebrows.

"Joni Sparkman, how dare you call astrology a lot of hocus-pocus?" she demanded.

"Because it—" Joni began.

"Hey, you two, knock it off," Crystal interrupted. "Look who's heading this way."

Joni glanced around to see Marissa and Cami wandering slowly through the crowded lunchroom, carrying their trays and looking around for somewhere to sit.

Joni waved to get their attention. "Marissa! Cami! Over here. We've got plenty of room." Then she leaned across the table and whispered to Crystal and Su-Su, "Here's our big chance. Let's make some room."

"See, *fate*!" Su-Su whispered back to Joni, grinning slyly as she scooted closer to Crystal.

"Gosh, thanks, guys," said Marissa. "It's really crowded in here today." She slid her tray onto the table and sat down on the bench across from Joni.

Cami nodded and smiled shyly, sitting down next to Marissa. "Yeah, thanks."

Joni glanced at the trays. Both girls had gotten the same lunches: chicken nuggets, macaroni and cheese, chocolate pudding, and milk.

Obviously Marissa had gone through the lunch line first and Cami had followed, making exactly the same selections.

Taking a bite out of the ham and cheese sandwich

she'd brought from home, Joni racked her brain for some way to bring up Todd's name. She knew it wasn't going to be easy. Marissa was picking glumly at her food, looking as if conversation was the last thing in the world she wanted. Cami never had much to say to begin with.

Su-Su and Crystal were strangely quiet, too. Joni figured they were probably trying to think of something brilliant to say, the same as she was.

Yikes! Joni thought. *If someone doesn't say something soon, lunch will be over, and we'll have missed our chance. Say something, anything.*

"Guess what I heard in Spanish this morning?" she practically shouted.

Everyone looked up, even Marissa.

"Hope Seymour told me that Ashley Malott talked her parents into letting her get a nose job!" said Joni. "Isn't that a scream?"

"Why would she want a nose job?" asked Crystal. "Her nose looks perfectly okay the way it is, if you ask me."

Joni shrugged. "Who knows?"

"Who *knows?*" Su-Su said, giggling. "Hey, that's funny, Sparkman. Get it, everybody?"

Everyone at the table laughed but Marissa. She was staring down into her plate again, poking at a chicken nugget with her fork.

When the laughter finally died down, the table

got even quieter than before.

We've blown it, Joni thought.

Just then Cami nudged Marissa. "Look, there's Todd," she said brightly. Without waiting for Marissa to say anything, she called out, "Hi, Todd! You can squeeze in with us."

Joni exchanged knowing glances with Su-Su and Crystal as Todd sat down between Marissa and Cami. He gave Marissa a quick grin and then turned to Cami.

"Hey, how's it going?"

Cami's huge brown eyes lit up. "Great. How about you?"

"Great," he said. Then, turning to the others at the table, he added, "Thanks for squeezing me in."

"No problem," said Joni, narrowing her eyes. It was easy to see why both girls could like the guy. He was good-looking with sandy hair and an athletic build, and he was always friendly to everybody. *Maybe too friendly,* Joni thought.

While everyone concentrated on lunch for the next few minutes, Joni kept an eye on Cami. She was looking down at her plate while she ate, but there was a tiny little smile on her face. Todd was devouring a chili dog and didn't seem to be paying attention to either girl, but Marissa darted nervous little glances toward him every now and again.

How obvious can you all get? Joni thought. *Marissa should be more than suspicious!*

Later, when Joni and Crystal and Su-Su were alone in the hall, all three of them started talking at once.

"Anyone with two eyes in their head can see what's going on," Joni huffed.

"Yeah, Todd sat right between them and said hi to Cami instead of Marissa," Su-Su said, angrily tossing her long red hair over one shoulder.

"It was disgusting," said Crystal. "Poor Marissa looked like she wanted to die."

"What I don't get is why she stays friends with Cami," said Joni. "Marissa's got to know what's going on."

"Maybe she really likes both of them," Crystal offered sadly.

Joni sighed. "And she called Boy Talk for help. I sure hope we can come through for her."

Chapter Six

"I've been racking my brain all afternoon and I haven't come up with one single solution for Marissa," Joni said with a sigh.

Su-Su, Joni, and Crystal were in Crystal's father's office after school, putting the Boy Talk tape into the answering machine.

"Me neither," said Crystal. "I really feel sorry for her, too." She checked her watch and turned on the answering machine. The telephone rang immediately.

Beep.

"Hi, Boy Talk. My friends keep telling me I'm boy-crazy, but *they're* the ones making me crazy. Every time I even mention a boy I think is cute or whenever I smile or flirt with a guy, they point it out and say, 'See, we told you. You're boy-crazy.' I just like boys, that's all. Does that make me boy-crazy? I'd really like to know. Call me Crazy."

"She certainly sounds boy-crazy to me," said Crystal.

"Why?" Su-Su asked. "She said she just likes boys." Then Su-Su got a sly smile on her face. "I remember when you were trying to get Evan Byrnes to like you. You talked about him constantly and flirted big-time every chance you got. Did that make you boy-crazy?"

Crystal looked indignant. "But that was just *one* boy. That was different."

The telephone rang again.

Beep.

"Hi, Boy Talk. I need some advice. There's this boy I really like. He comes over sometimes, but he never asks me out. Last night when he came over, he showed me this list of the girls he likes, and I'm his *third choice*. I want to be first! What can I do to make him like me better? Call me Third-Rate."

"What a jerk!" Joni said when Third-Rate hung up. "He has a lot of nerve putting her down that way. What does she see in him?"

"I agree," said Su-Su.

"Speaking of put-downs, if you ask me, Cami and Todd's flirting in front of Marissa in the cafeteria today must have been a real bummer for Marissa," said Crystal. "Maybe we should tell her to break up with him and save her pride."

Joni shook her head. "We can't do that. It would only make her more miserable."

"Yeah, and give Todd and Cami the perfect excuse to get together," added Su-Su.

The telephone rang again, but no one left a message after the beep. It happened a second and a third time as kids called in just to listen. After the fourth beep, someone finally spoke.

Beep.

"Hey, Third-Rate, listen up. You probably don't realize it, but you like this guy because he's a big challenge. I'll bet you wouldn't find him half as interesting if he didn't have that list, and he knows it. Playing hard to get is his little game. Wouldn't you rather be first on a new guy's list? I sure would. Just call me List-Less."

List-Less had barely hung up when another call came in.

Beep.

"Hi, Boy Talk. This is a message for Crazy. Do you daydream about boys all the time? Do you giggle about them with your friends? Do you notice every single thing about them—what they're wearing, what they look like, how they act—and rate them according to which ones you like best? Do you pass notes about guys in class? Get up an hour early so you'll look great at school? Walk out of your way to pass a guy's house or take a different route to class—even if it makes you late—to see him? Those are just a few of the symptoms of being boy-crazy. I know because I have them all! Call me Lovesick."

Crystal turned to Su-Su. "See! I didn't do all those things over Evan."

"Whaaaaat?" shrieked Su-Su. "Who are you trying to kid? You did every one of them."

"Well, what about you and Chris Oberlin?" Crystal retorted. "You went absolutely bonkers over that guy. You even wrote a fake love note to yourself from Chris."

Su-Su's face turned as red as her hair, but the phone rang again before she could think of a come-back.

"Saved by the bell," Joni told her, grinning.

Beep.

"Hi, Boy Talk. I have a message for Crazy. You sound pretty far gone to me, but so what? There's nothing you can do about it anyway. The more you try *not* to think about boys, the more you will. The next time your friends tell you you're boy-crazy, just say, 'Big deal.' That's what I did. I'm Boy-Crazy Too."

"I think Boy-Crazy Too had the best advice," said Su-Su. "Everybody should just leave Crazy alone and let her be boy-crazy if that's what she wants."

Joni sighed when Boy-Crazy Too hung up. "All

the girls who called in today really have trivial problems compared to Suspicious and His Secret Love, don't they?"

"Well, yeah," said Crystal. "But they seem like big problems to them, I guess."

"Has anybody thought of any really good advice to give Suspicious yet?" asked Joni. "I'm getting worried. We can't let her down. She needs us."

Crystal and Su-Su shook their heads.

Just then the phone rang again.

Beep.

"Hi, Boy Talk. This is Suspicious again. I really appreciate the girl who said she was Whoopi Goldberg calling in and saying I was overpossessive and I should relax, but ..." The caller sniffled.

"It's Marissa!" Crystal shouted when the voice paused.

"And she sounds awful," added Su-Su.

There was a big sigh on the tape. Finally Suspicious went on. "Anyway, her advice didn't work for me. It's too late for any more advice for Suspicious. I have a new name now—*Double Dumped.*"

Chapter Seven

"Oh, no!" Joni murmured.

Joni, Crystal, and Su-Su hovered over the answering machine in horrified silence as Double Dumped continued.

"Last night my boyfriend called me and said he wanted to break up. I asked him why, and he said he liked someone else. Then I asked him who, and"—she sniffed back tears—"he said it was *my best friend!*"

Joni could hear Marissa crying. Her heart ached for her.

"How could she do such a thing?" Marissa went on. "I mean, we've been friends for almost forever. And she's always been so shy. I even asked my boyfriend to pay extra attention to her because she gets all nervous whenever boys try to talk to her. That was my big mistake."

She paused, and Joni heard her gulp back tears again.

"Anyway, he was real nice to her, and I thought everything was great until lately when he started acting cool to me. I could tell he was being extra-friendly to her, but I didn't want to believe the truth. I was only trying to help her out, and she stole my boyfriend! How can I get him back?"

"Pond scum," Su-Su muttered when the tape ended. "Cami and Todd are both pond scum. How could they do a thing like that to poor Marissa? I think she's nuts to want him back."

"I sort of know how she feels," Joni said slowly. She couldn't help thinking about Beau and what an important part of her life he was. "Remember how upset I was when I thought Beau was sneaking around with Megan Scully? I was furious at him, but I would have done practically anything to get him back."

"I guess you're right," said Su-Su. "Chris has never done anything like that, but I know how I'd feel if he did."

"I think we should go straight over to Marissa's house when Boy Talk is over and give her three shoulders to cry on," said Crystal.

"We can't do that," said Joni. "We have to keep

our identities a secret, remember? That's the only way Boy Talk will work."

Crystal sighed. "I know. I just forgot for a minute."

"Well, I hope Cami calls back in and hears what she's done to Marissa," grumbled Su-Su. "If that doesn't give her a guilty conscience, nothing will."

"Cami won't call again," said Joni. "Why should she? She doesn't need advice anymore. She's got Todd."

All Joni could think about the rest of the afternoon was how much Marissa was hurting. As they were leaving Crystal's, she said, "You know, guys, we should be extra-friendly to Marissa at school tomorrow. We'll have to be super-careful not to let on that we know she's Double Dumped, but we can still be there for her if she needs us."

"Oh, Joni, that's a great idea," said Crystal, smiling so wide that her dimple appeared like magic. "She probably won't be hanging around with Cami, that's for sure."

"Yeah," said Su-Su. "We'll put on a good act. Marissa will never suspect we know the whole story."

Crystal and Su-Su promised to meet Joni at her locker as soon as they could the next morning. That way they'd be there when Marissa got to hers.

Joni arrived at school first, but within five minutes Crystal and Su-Su were standing beside her at her locker.

"It's still half an hour until the bell, but I'm already getting nervous," said Crystal.

"Whatever you do, don't let it show," Joni cautioned. "We've got to chill so she doesn't suspect anything."

"We should have planned what to say," Crystal said. "What if one of us blows it, like me?" Her eyes were wide with worry.

"Chill out, Crystal. We'll think of something to say when Marissa gets here," said Su-Su. "Trust me. If all else fails, I brought my trusty horoscope." She whipped a folded sheet of newspaper out of her notebook and waved it in the air. "It never fails."

Joni and Crystal both groaned. "In fact," Su-Su went on, ignoring them, "I read all three of ours for today.

"Okay, Crystal, you're a Cancer. Here's yours: 'Unfortunately, wishing will not make things happen today. If you want something special, you must work extra-hard to get it.'"

"Isn't that what we're trying to do right now?" Crystal asked. "We're wishing Marissa felt better, but we're trying to help her, too."

"Get real, Crystal. Don't you know you can interpret those star things any way you want to?" said Joni.

"Listen up, Scorpio," Su-Su said. She pointed a finger at Joni. "'Your friends may express interest in what you have to say today, but be careful not to monopolize every conversation.' No kidding. That's really what it says." She broke up laughing.

Joni reached for the paper. "Let me see that. I think you're making it up."

Su-Su handed her the page with an air of triumph. She watched with glee as Joni read the exact words she had just read out loud. "So you'll believe me next time?" asked Su-Su, taking back the paper.

"You'll believe what next time?" asked a voice from behind them.

When they all turned around, Joni saw in surprise that it was Marissa. She was smiling as if she didn't have a care in the world.

"It sounded pretty mysterious, whatever you were talking about," Marissa added. She began to work the combination on her locker.

"Su-Su's a horoscope freak," said Joni, glaring at Su-Su. "She was reading ours to us so we'll know how to behave today."

Marissa raised one brow. "I don't need any horoscope to tell me how to act today," she said happily. "I've already got plans. I might as well tell you why, since you'll find out soon anyway. I broke up with Todd last night."

Joni stared at her in amazement. "You did? I mean, you look so... so happy."

"I *am* happy," Marissa said. A big smile stretched

across her face. "Why wouldn't I be? *I* broke up with *him*. I've been wanting to for a long time. I mean, he was getting so *boring*. But I kept putting it off because I didn't want to hurt him. Finally I couldn't stand it any longer, so when he called last night, I gave him the bad news. Boy, do I feel better!"

"Congratulations," said Su-Su, nodding. "Even if he's hurt, he's cute and popular. He'll probably find somebody new."

Joni gave her friend a sharp nudge. What a stupid thing to say!

But Marissa had already pulled her books out of her locker and shut it. "He already has," she said. Heading down the hall, she called back over her shoulder, "I fixed him up with Cami. They're perfect for each other."

Joni, Crystal, and Su-Su stared after her in stunned silence. When she was almost too far away to hear, Su-Su yelled, "Hey, Marissa! When's your birthday?"

Marissa stopped and looked back. "April sixth, but I don't believe in that horoscope stuff." Then she turned and went on down the hall.

"Why do you want to read Marissa's horoscope?" Joni asked Su-Su. "Either the girl is lying or she isn't Double Dumped after all." Su-Su didn't answer. She was studying the horoscope page again.

"Here it is," she said. "Aries: 'Today you might be tempted to point the finger of blame at the wrong person. Don't forget, the truth always comes out sooner or later.'"

Chapter Eight

"Why is Marissa faking being happy?" asked Crystal as she, Joni, and Su-Su strolled through the hall toward their first-period classes.

"You'd think she'd want all the sympathy she can get," said Su-Su. "I certainly would."

"I think I know how Marissa feels," said Joni. "She's really hurt and needs advice. That's why she called Boy Talk. But she'd probably die of embarrassment if any kids who heard her message figured out who she was. Her pride is hurt, that's all."

Crystal sighed. "You could be right, but that just makes it a whole lot harder for us to help her. If there was some way we could get her to talk to us in person and tell us more about what happened, maybe we could get more of a clue about what to do."

"Right now I think we should be on the lookout for Todd and Cami so we can see how they're acting," said Joni. "Don't let them catch you watching them, though."

"So now you've got *us* playing detective," said Su-Su with a laugh.

"Right," said Joni. She stopped by the door to her Spanish class. "I'll meet you guys at noon."

She didn't see either Cami or Todd until third period. Cami was in her science class. Joni sat four seats behind Cami and one row over. It was perfect for spying without being seen.

Cami was one of the last to come into the classroom. She sauntered in with a faraway look in her big brown eyes, hugging her books.

Aha! thought Joni. *She's thinking about Todd.*

Joni tingled with excitement. None of the Lindsey Jones mysteries that she loved to read had a plot that was anything like Double Dumped's problem, but in almost all of the books Lindsey kept an eye on someone while she looked for clues.

Soon the room was abuzz with kids talking about the big test tomorrow, but Cami wasn't paying attention to anyone. She kept chewing on a strand of dark hair and gazing toward the windows.

Had Todd called her after he broke up with Marissa last night? Joni wondered. *Had he told her what had happened and asked her to go out with him officially? It* was impossible to tell just by looking whether Cami was in a daze because she had finally gotten the guy she wanted or if she was still wishing.

When the bell rang, Mrs. Simon, the science teacher, began going over the review questions that she had handed out for yesterday's homework. Joni tried to listen and check her answers, but she couldn't get her mind off Cami.

How could anyone get so carried away over a boy that she would take him away from her best friend? Joni wondered. Could Marissa and Cami ever be friends again?

When Joni, Crystal, and Su-Su met in the cafeteria at noon, no one had anything special to report.

"Todd was in my health class, but he just looked normal," Su-Su said with a shrug.

"I didn't see either one of them," said Crystal. "Not even in the halls."

Joni told her friends about watching Cami in science class and being unable to tell if she had talked to Todd since the breakup or not.

"Of course he called her," Su-Su said. "The two of them probably planned out how he was going to break up with Marissa ahead of time."

"What we really need is to see them together," Joni mused. She glanced around the crowded lunchroom. "I don't see them in here now."

"What difference does it make?" asked Su-Su.

"How is seeing the two of them as a couple going to help Marissa get Todd back?"

"A good detective evaluates the whole situation," Joni explained patiently. "Who knows? Maybe things between Cami and Todd aren't what they seem."

Crystal got a puzzled look on her face. "You mean, maybe they don't really like each other? Then why would Todd break up with Marissa and tell her he liked Cami?"

"I don't know," Joni said, sighing in frustration. "I just know that when Beau and I had our problem, things didn't turn out to be as bad as they seemed. Maybe Marissa will be just as lucky, too."

"Hey, look!" said Su-Su, pointing across the room. "There's Todd sitting at the same table with Beau, Twister, Parker, and Jason. I don't see Cami anywhere."

"I do," Joni said. She craned her neck to look over the crowd. "She's paying for her lunch right now. And guess what else?"

"What?" Su-Su and Crystal said in unison.

"Marissa isn't around," said Joni. "Cami's by herself."

"You can't expect them to be buddy-buddy if Cami just stole Todd," Crystal said. "Marissa's probably in here somewhere, sitting with someone else."

"Maybe she's with Ashley and Hope," said Su-Su.

"The three of them do things together sometimes."

Joni stood up and made a careful check of every table. Marissa wasn't sitting with Ashley and Hope. She wasn't sitting at any table. She wasn't in line for hot lunch, either. Then Joni glanced out the window and did a double take. "Uh-oh, guys. I've found her," said Joni. "She's outside, sitting by herself on the steps. And guess what? She's crying."

Su-Su jumped up to look. "Poor Marissa," she said. "And it's all Cami's fault."

"You bet," Joni muttered. She was starting to dislike Cami Petre more with every passing minute.

"I hate to tell you this," Crystal said softly. "But look where Cami's sitting."

Joni glanced around to where Crystal was looking and drew her breath in sharply. "She's sitting with Todd, all right!" Joni said angrily. "With Todd and Twister and Parker and Jason and *Beau*!"

Her blood started to boil as she watched Cami give Beau a big smile and say something to him. Beau looked self-conscious at first, but he shrugged and smiled back. Then Cami turned her attention to Jason, who seemed really pleased, and then back to Beau again.

"She sure isn't shy anymore," Su-Su said.

Crystal nodded. "You can say that again. Look, she's cozying up to Twister, of all people! Ugh. And she's batting her eyes!"

"It's disgusting," Su-Su agreed. "Look at that! She's got all five boys practically eating out of her hand."

"That little flirt," Joni muttered. "She'd better not think she can make a habit of stealing other girls' boyfriends. And she'd *better* not think she can steal Beau!"

Joni kept an eye on Cami while she nibbled on her sandwich. She was greatly relieved when Cami finally stopped flirting and started eating her lunch.

"You'd better do something in case she does go after Beau," said Su-Su.

"Oh, I'm going to do something, all right," Joni said confidently. "I'm going to help Marissa get Todd back if it's the last thing I do. *Then* I'll take care of Cami."

Chapter Nine

Joni fumed over Cami for the rest of the day. She couldn't get the picture out of her mind of the flirty way Cami had smiled at Beau. Of course Beau had only half-smiled back, but that didn't excuse Cami. She was definitely the enemy now. And what made Joni extra mad was that Cami had always been cute, with her enormous brown eyes and long dark hair, but she had been so shy that no one ever really noticed her—until now.

She hurried to her locker after school, hoping she could catch Marissa before she left. She was in luck. Marissa was just picking up her knapsack.

"Hi, Marissa," Joni said.

She waited for Marissa to look up before she went on. "I saw Todd and Cami in the cafeteria together today," she said.

Marissa's face was expressionless, but Joni thought she saw a slight flicker in her eyes.

"To tell you the truth, I'm not sure those two are right for each other," Joni went on. "And for someone who used to be shy, Cami sure knows how to flirt."

"Cami? Flirting?" Marissa murmured.

Joni could tell she was genuinely surprised. *Good,* thought Joni. *I can't let her give up hope that Cami and Todd will break up, but I need some time while I sabotage their little romance.*

"You bet she was flirting," Joni said aloud. "And one of the boys she was flirting with was my boyfriend."

"Beau?" Marissa asked in astonishment. "Cami Petre was flirting with *Beau Maguire?*"

"Hey, are you guys talking about me?" Beau stopped beside Joni's locker and gave her a quizzical look.

Joni smiled conspiratorially at Marissa. "We'll never tell."

Marissa smiled back. "Go ahead and torture us, but our lips are sealed!"

Beau leaned against Joni's open locker door. "Hey, do you still want to study for the science test together? It's tomorrow, you know."

"Sure," said Joni. "And I know it's tomorrow, believe me. I'm still not ready."

"Let's go to your house right now and hit the books," said Beau.

Joni gulped. "Now? Why don't you come over after supper like you always do?"

Beau shrugged. "Can't. There's another basketball game at the Y tonight. What's wrong with right now?"

Joni's mind was racing. She couldn't tell Beau that she had to go to Crystal's for Boy Talk. But what could she say? "I have to go to the doctor," she blurted out. It was the first thing that came to her mind.

Beau looked concerned. "The doctor? Are you sick?"

"Um, no. It's just a checkup. My parents are real fanatics about making sure Hannah and I get regular checkups," said Joni. She knew the whole excuse sounded stupid, but she was too rattled to think up something else.

"So how long will your checkup take?" asked Beau. "I mean, I could ride my bike to your house and be there when you get home."

Eeeek! thought Joni. She couldn't let him do that. He'd find out she was lying for sure.

"I don't know how long I'll be. It'll depend on if they take me right away. You know how doctors' offices are," she said. Then without thinking, she added, "If it wasn't for your dumb basketball game, we could study after supper!"

Joni was sorry the instant the words were out of her mouth.

Anger flashed in Beau's eyes. "Basketball isn't dumb," he muttered. Then he turned and walked away.

Tears blurred Joni's eyes as she watched him leave. Marissa looked at her sympathetically.

"I'm the one who's dumb," Joni whispered to herself. "I did it again. I opened my big mouth without thinking. And now I may have played right into Cami Petre's hands."

Chapter Ten

Joni poured out the whole horrible story of what had happened at her locker to Crystal and Su-Su as they set up the Boy Talk tape.

"Beau is definitely mad at me now," said Joni. "And in a way, I don't blame him. I don't know what comes over me sometimes. I keep letting my emotions get in my way and I blurt out stupid things."

Crystal's eyes were full of pity. "I know how you feel. I do that sometimes, too. I guess everybody our age does."

"I have crazy mood swings you wouldn't believe," Su-Su said. "Especially when my brother, Patrick, is around."

"Cami Petre is going to make me crazy," said Joni.

"What has come over that girl, anyway?" Su-Su

asked. "She was always so shy. And why would she want to go after anybody else now that she's got Todd?"

"Maybe Todd is the first boy who's really paid much attention to her, and it's given her self-confidence she never had before," suggested Crystal.

"Well, she'd just better stay away from Chris," grumbled Su-Su.

"Let's forget about Cami right now and think about Marissa," said Joni. "We've got to come up with a way for her to get Todd back."

"I'm thinking, I'm thinking," Su-Su insisted. "But let's face it, I've *gotten* a boyfriend. I don't have any idea how to get one *back*."

"Me neither," Crystal said glumly.

Joni sighed. "Let's keep our fingers crossed that *someone* calls in with some really good advice."

The telephone started ringing at three thirty-one.

Beep.

"Hi, Boy Talk. This is advice for Double Dumped from Disgusted. Forget both of them. A boyfriend who sneaks around with his girlfriend's best friend is scum, and with a best friend like her, you don't need enemies."

Beep.

"Double Dumped, this is a message from Get Real. And I mean it! Why would you want him back, anyway? He'd probably just break your heart again."

Beep.

"Hi, Boy Talk. This is Thief of Hearts calling again, and I'm leaving a message for Double Dumped. I called in when you were still just Suspicious, remember? Well, now that you've been dumped, I've got the perfect advice for you. Get even! All boys are fair game. Pick out one that you'd like to go after and flirt your head off. If he's got a girlfriend, so what?"

"What!" Joni rose off her chair when Thief of Hearts hung up. "That's rotten advice! In fact, everyone who's called in so far has given rotten advice."

"Not really," Su-Su said. "Marissa probably *would* be happier without Todd, especially if she could find someone else."

"Don't tell *her* that," said Joni. "She doesn't want anybody else. She wants Todd back, and we're going to help her."

She sank slowly back into her chair and stared at the answering machine. Suddenly the perfect solution hit her. Everybody at school—boys included—thought Cami was so nice and so shy. Well, she wasn't like that anymore. What would they think if they saw her for what she really was? A sneaky, low-down person who was trying super-hard to get every boy in school to fall for her!

Running into Crystal's room, she punched in the Boy Talk number on the other phone.

Su-Su followed her and stood in the doorway with a puzzled look on her face. "What are you doing?" she asked.

"Listen and you'll find out," said Joni as the greeting came on.

Beep.

"Hi, Boy Talk. I'm recording a message for Double Dumped," she said, holding her nose to disguise her voice. "I know exactly what you should do about your *ex*–best friend. Start a smear campaign so that everyone else will find out what kind of person she really is. You don't have to lie. Just tell the truth about her and how she's flirting now with every boy around. Then your old boyfriend will probably dump her, and nobody else will come near her. You'll get your boyfriend back, and she'll be sorry."

Out of the corner of her eye, Joni could see Su-Su's mouth drop open.

"Just call me In the Know," Joni said and hung up.

"Joni, I can't believe you said that," Su-Su said.

"I can't, either," said Crystal, hurrying in from her father's office.

"Why not? You saw Cami flirting with Beau and those other guys," Joni said defensively. "And I'll bet she'd flirt with Evan and Chris, too, if she got half a chance."

"But a smear campaign," Crystal said, shaking her head, "that's going a little far. And you said those *other* girls gave bad advice."

"But don't you get it? Todd will realize that Marissa is a much nicer person than Cami, and they'll get back together," Joni said pleadingly. "And Cami will leave …" Her voice trailed off as tears filled her throat. *Beau alone*, she finished silently.

The phone on the answering machine rang. Without a word Su-Su and Crystal headed back.

Joni stood beside Crystal's desk, feeling as if her world was falling apart. She wanted to help Marissa out. But her own emotions kept getting in the way. Now it wasn't just Beau who was mad at her. Her best friends were angry, too.

Chapter Eleven

The next day was Friday, the day of the killer science test. Joni had been way too miserable to study on Thursday night. All she could think about was all the trouble her big mouth had gotten her into.

Su-Su and Crystal hadn't mentioned her message to Double Dumped again, but they had been awfully quiet—both for the rest of Boy Talk yesterday and now at school. It was obvious that they thought she'd made a major mistake.

As third period began, Joni sank into her seat in the science room and watched in fascination as Cami Petre flirted with Jordan Losen two rows over. Cami kept opening her eyes really wide at Jordan. Then she'd tilt her head and give him a big smile. Jordan was eating it up. He gave her a dopey grin, and Joni could see the edges of his ears turning red.

How did she learn all that so fast? Joni wondered. Maybe Cami had been watching other girls flirt for a long time, waiting to get up enough nerve to try their techniques.

As soon as the bell rang and Mrs. Simon handed out the test papers, Joni was sorry she had let her love life distract her from studying. She glanced down the double row of questions and groaned to herself. This test was *hard.*

Joni couldn't believe how fast the period went by. She sweated over every question and was still working on the last one when the bell rang again and Mrs. Simon called for the papers to be passed forward.

She was heading toward the door, feeling like a zombie, when she heard a girl behind her say, "Hey, Cami, did you hear what Marissa Pauley is saying about you?"

"Marissa's talking about me? What did she say?" Cami demanded.

Joni immediately perked up, trying to hear the rest of the conversation, but Jordan Losen and a couple of other boys pushed in behind her, wedging themselves between her and Cami and the girl Cami was talking to.

My plan is working! Joni thought with satisfaction. *Marissa, aka Double Dumped, took my advice!* Todd would be sure to hear the word about Cami soon. Gossip spread fast around Sunshine Beach Middle School.

Joni felt a twinge of guilt. Usually she hated gossip. *But this isn't really gossip*, she argued with herself. *Gossip means telling lies. This is the truth!*

By the time Joni reached the cafeteria for lunch, she had heard from three different girls that Cami Petre had turned into a boy-crazy flirt.

"She told me that Marissa Pauley and Todd Merrill broke up and Todd was *her* boyfriend now," said Hope Seymour as she and Joni entered the lunch room together. "But I saw her zoning in on Alex Ranson in English class. Boy, has she changed."

Hope peeled off toward the hot-lunch line, and Joni looked around for Crystal and Su-Su. They were sitting at a table near the back of the room, not far from where Cami was snuggled up close to Todd, feeding him a potato chip.

"Did you catch *that?*" Joni asked as she dropped her lunch bag on the table and nodded toward Cami and Todd.

"Couldn't miss it," Su-Su replied. "It makes me want to throw up."

"I don't think Cami realizes she's making a fool of herself," said Crystal. "She'd better slow down or she'll get an awful reputation."

Joni glanced at Cami again. Cami was gazing adoringly at Todd. Joni felt another wave of guilt. She probably shouldn't have encouraged Marissa to talk about Cami like that. From the looks of things, Cami was going to look boy-crazy enough without anyone else's help.

Joni shuddered. She really hoped Cami kept her big brown eyes off Beau. She hadn't even talked to him since their fight. And he had totally ignored her in science class. She hoped it was because he was nervous about the test.

"So how do you think you did on the science test?" asked Crystal. "I thought it was hard."

"I don't think I did that well," Joni admitted. "In fact I think it was awful. I guess I was so busy worrying about Marissa and Cami and Todd and Beau that I didn't study the way I usually do."

"Thanks for the good news, guys," said Su-Su. "You know I don't have that test until this afternoon. Now I'm scared out of my mind."

"Don't worry. You'll ace it," Joni assured her. "You're good in science."

She was about to take a bite out of her apple when she spotted Beau and Twister carrying their lunch trays through the crowd.

Don't you dare go near Cami Petre, Joni warned him silently.

Twister slid his tray across an empty table, and Beau followed. Joni breathed a sigh of relief. Then she saw Beau look back over his shoulder at Cami and Todd. An instant later he jumped up and went over to talk to them.

"What is he doing? That little flirt! She's after him again, I just know it," Joni said angrily. "Look at that!"

Su-Su and Crystal looked where Joni was pointing.

"Maybe Todd called him over, not Cami," offered Crystal.

"Right," Joni said sarcastically.

Beau didn't stay long at Todd and Cami's table. He scooted back to his own a few minutes later and began devouring his lunch.

Joni took a last bite out of her apple and threw it into her lunch bag. Suddenly she'd lost her appetite.

"I'm finished if you guys are," she told Su-Su and Crystal.

As the three of them got up to leave, Joni glanced toward Beau again. He was watching her.

"Hey, Joni," he called out over the noise of the crowd. "Come here a sec." He waved, and Joni's heart jumped.

"You guys go ahead. I'll catch up," she said to her friends.

Joni was almost afraid of what Beau was going to say. He had been talking to Todd and Cami a minute before, and she had no idea what to expect from

Cami anymore. It could be something awful.

She stopped beside his table, feeling awkward. "Hi, Beau. What's up?"

Beau took a gulp of milk and swiped his mouth with the back of his hand before he answered.

"Todd and Cami want us to double with them to the movie tonight," he said. "I said okay."

Joni did a double take. "What?" she asked incredulously.

"We go to the movies every Friday night," Beau said, frowning. "And I thought you liked Cami. Anyway, I already told them we would."

"Oh, um, sure," Joni said, fumbling for words. At least Beau wasn't mad at her anymore. "It sounds great."

Actually, it sounded terrible. Would everyone think she was Cami's friend now and not Marissa's? And what would Marissa think?

Joni knew she'd have to get a grip on herself. Otherwise, she'd never survive the double date.

Chapter Twelve

Joni fidgeted nervously in the backseat beside Beau as Mr. Maguire drove them to the movie theater that evening. Her mind was spinning as she tried to imagine what double-dating with Todd Merrill and Cami Petre was going to be like. She couldn't picture it at all!

Beau had started talking about the basketball tournament and his star performance the moment she got into the car, but if he noticed that Joni was extra quiet, he didn't show it. "And then I stole the ball from Twister and tore down the court for a slam dunk," he was bragging when Joni tuned back in. "You should have been there. I was sooo awesome!"

"Yeah, I bet," she murmured and quickly went

back to worrying about what she'd say to Cami when they met face-to-face.

She didn't have long to wait. Friday night was the date night of the week, and most Sunshine Beach middle schoolers went to the movies. The sidewalk in front of Cinema Six was crowded with kids when Mr. Maguire dropped them off a few minutes later. They bought tickets and headed into the large lobby that served all six screening rooms.

"Come on, here they are," said Beau, taking Joni's arm and steering her through the crowd.

Todd had just paid for a large tub of popcorn and two drinks, and he and Cami were leaving the snack bar.

"Hey, Merrill!" Beau called. "Wait up."

Both Todd and Cami stopped and looked around. Joni thought Cami looked prettier than usual. She had used a curling iron to give her normally straight dark hair soft waves around her face, and she was wearing a gorgeous pale blue sweater.

Joni held her breath as Cami's eyes lit up and a big smile broke over her face. She glanced quickly at Beau and then zeroed in on Joni as they approached.

"Hi, Joni," she said sweetly. "I'm so glad we're doubling tonight." Then she hooked her arm through Todd's and looked up at him adoringly. "It's going to be so much fun, isn't it, Todd?"

Joni wanted to throw up. But instead she smiled

weakly and nodded. She hated the lovesick look on Cami's face. It was embarrassing to be seen with someone who acted like that. Joni turned away and glanced around at the crowd, trying to look anywhere other than at Cami.

Her gaze stopped abruptly as her eyes suddenly locked with Marissa Pauley's. The blond girl was standing near the ticket taker's stand at the end of the hallway leading to the theaters. Hurt was written all over her face. Hope and Ashley beside her were looking at Joni, too, but their expressions were ones of total disgust.

Joni swallowed hard. She wanted to rush over to Marissa and explain that doubling with Cami and Todd hadn't been her idea, that she'd rather be almost anywhere else in the world at that exact moment. She wanted to tell all three of them that she and Su-Su and Crystal were trying their best to help Marissa, no matter how it looked right now.

"Hey, Joni, what did you think of that science test today?" Cami asked from behind her. "I thought it was a real killer, didn't you?"

Joni looked down at the floor. She didn't want to turn around and answer Cami. Not right now, with Marissa and her friends looking on.

"Earth to Joni," Cami said, "did you hear me? I asked what you thought of the science test."

Slowly Joni turned around. She knew Marissa was

watching her, but there was nothing else she could do. "Yeah, it was pretty brutal," Joni said. She darted another quick glance toward Marissa just in time to see the blond girl tilt her chin upward and walk away, with Hope and Ashley following her.

I guess I know what they think of me now, Joni thought sadly.

"You guys thought that test was hard?" Beau asked. "I'm sure I aced it. I really studied hard."

There was a hint of sarcasm in his voice, and Joni knew it was for her benefit. She suddenly felt as if she was being bombarded from all sides. Beau was still mad that she had called his basketball tournament stupid and then had refused to study with him Thursday afternoon. Marissa was hurt because Joni was out with Cami and Todd, and Ashley and Hope were on Marissa's side.

"Knock it off, will you?" she muttered to Beau. "I told you I had a doctor's appointment on Thursday."

Cami had been watching them. Now she opened her big brown eyes wide and leaned toward Beau. "It's almost time for the movie to start," she said, touching him on the arm. "Don't you think we should go in?"

Joni did a slow burn as Beau flashed Cami a big smile. "Yeah, sure," he said. He started moving toward the ticket taker with Cami beside him. Neither of them even looked back to see if Joni and Todd were following them.

It took them a while to find four seats together, but when they did, Cami pushed Todd into the row ahead of her and made sure Beau was right behind her, with Joni bringing up the rear. "Boy-girl, boy-girl," she said, laughing.

Joni wanted to protest, but she knew she would only look jealous if she did. She sighed in disgust and sat down on the end. She half listened as Cami chattered happily to Todd and Beau about something cute her dog had done the day before. Cami was the center of attention, and Joni had a feeling she was being left out on purpose.

Suddenly something soft grazed the top of her head and fell into her lap. It was a wadded-up paper napkin, and Joni could see that something was written on it in red ink. Unfolding it, Joni read the message.

Wait until the movie starts, then meet us in the ladies' room.

Crystal and Su-Su

P.S. We're two rows behind you.

Joni grinned to herself as the lights went down. She should have known her friends would come through for her. Help was on the way!

Chapter Thirteen

Joni had never felt more relieved in her life. She had known that Su-Su and Crystal were going to the movies with Chris and Evan tonight, but she hadn't seen them in the lobby. And last she'd heard, the four of them hadn't decided which movie to see.

As soon as the coming attractions were over and the feature came on, Joni jumped out of her seat and made her way up the aisle. Crystal and Su-Su were waiting when she pushed open the door to the empty ladies' room.

"What's going on?" Su-Su asked excitedly.

"Tell us absolutely everything," begged Crystal. "We're *dying* of suspense!"

"What's going on? Not much," Joni said with a snort. "Cami's got Todd wrapped around her little finger and now she's throwing herself at Beau. 'Boy-girl, boy-girl,'" she mimicked in a high-pitched voice. Then she went on to tell her friends more about Cami's annoying behavior.

"We thought something like that was going on," Crystal said grimly. "We were keeping an eye on you guys, and it definitely looked like bad news."

"Speaking of bad news, we overheard Marissa talking to Ashley and Hope in the lobby," said Su-Su. She ran a finger across her throat. "She's really mad at you. She told them she had always thought you were her friend, but now she knows the truth and she hates your guts."

"That's just *great*," muttered Joni, rolling her eyes in despair. She sighed and leaned against a sink. "We're trying everything we can think of to help her get Todd back, and she hates my guts!"

"Obviously, she doesn't know that you're trying to help," Crystal reasoned. "She even thi—"

She shut up immediately as April Mathis and Molly Triola came into the rest room. The two seemed surprised to see them there, but then April's face lit up.

"Hi, guys. Taking time out from the movie for a gossip break?" she asked, giving them a knowing look.

Joni's heart sank. Outside of Cami Petre, April Mathis was the last person on earth she wanted to see right then. April was the captain of the cheer-leading squad and the undisputed leader of the most popular clique at school. She always had to know everything that was going on, and could be counted on to pry into everybody's business. She and her friends had also been trying to find out who was behind Boy Talk ever since the hot line had started. A few times she had come very, very close.

"As a matter of fact, we were just leaving," said Joni. "Come on," she added, motioning to Crystal and Su-Su, "we'd better get back. We don't want to miss the movie."

"You don't think they heard anything we were saying, do you?" asked Crystal when they were safely back out in the hallway.

"That's *all* we need," muttered Su-Su.

"I don't think so," said Joni. "But we'd better be extra-careful what we say and where we say it from now on."

When Joni scooted into the row and sat down beside Beau again, he didn't even look up. He and Cami and Todd were whispering together instead of watching the movie.

He didn't even realize I was gone, Joni thought as tears misted her eyes. *Or care!*

She sank down deeper in her seat and stared up at the screen. It could have been blank for all she knew. She didn't even have a clue as to what was going on in the movie.

Maybe we should just give up Boy Talk. Look what it's doing to me, she thought miserably. *We should just forget about other kids and their problems. Why don't we stop trying to help everybody else and just concentrate on ourselves?*

Joni knew she was wallowing in self-pity, but she couldn't help it. She couldn't think about anything else. Her world was falling apart. And all her troubles had started with Boy Talk.

"Hey, wake up! The show's over."

Joni glanced up to see Beau staring down at her. The screen was dark, the lights were on, and people were filing out of the theater.

"Did you have a good nap?" he asked with a chuckle.

Joni jumped to her feet. She could feel her face turning bright red. "I wasn't sleeping!" she snapped. "I was thinking about something. Something really important."

Beau shrugged. "If you say so." He didn't even ask what the important thing was.

Mr. Maguire was waiting in the car when they got outside. Joni climbed in without a word, and she and Beau rode home in silence.

"Thanks, Mr. Maguire," she said when she got out.

She hesitated a few seconds, figuring Beau would get out and walk her to the door the way he usually did. He didn't budge.

"I'll see you," he said.

"Right," Joni murmured. She closed the car door and walked slowly up the front walk.

She had the awful feeling that Marissa Pauley might not be the only one who'd been dumped.

Chapter Fourteen

Joni was at home cleaning up the lunch dishes the next day when she heard the doorbell ring. She had spent most of the morning on the phone, pouring out her troubles to Crystal and Su-Su, but they hadn't been able to do much except listen and sympathize.

Now she pricked up her ears in surprise when she heard her father say, "Why, hello, Beau. Come on in. Joni's in the kitchen."

Joni grabbed a towel and dried her hands, but she was almost afraid to turn around when she heard Beau come into the room. Was this it? Had he come over to tell her he wanted to break up?

Just then Hannah, Joni's six-year-old sister, came

skipping into the room. She broke into a big grin when she saw Beau.

"Hi, Beau!" she cried. "Wanna play a game? I just got a new one called—"

"Hannah! Stop being a pest," Joni interrupted. "Beau didn't come over to see *you*." Then, thinking she might have said the wrong thing, she looked at Beau and added meekly, "Did you?"

Beau shook his head. "Sorry, Hannah. I need to talk to Joni. I'll play a game with you next time."

Joni watched Hannah scuff out of the room in disappointment. She was still too nervous to look Beau in the eye.

"I need to talk to you, Joni," he said. "I have to ask you something."

"Sure," she said. Her pulse pounded in her ears as loudly as the surf at the beach during a storm. "What do you want to know?"

"Oh, hi, Beau," said her mother, frowning as she walked into the kitchen. "Joni, have you seen the sewing scissors? I can't find them anywhere."

Joni shook her head, and her mother started rummaging through all the kitchen drawers.

"Um, maybe we could go someplace else," suggested Beau. "How about riding our bikes to the beach?"

"Okay," said Joni, but that idea didn't make her feel any better. It was obvious that whatever Beau wanted to ask her was pretty private—and pretty important.

It was a warm and sunny Saturday afternoon as they pedaled through town and locked their bikes in the bike rack at the edge of the walkway leading to the public beach.

Beau had hardly said a word during the entire fifteen-minute ride, and Joni was about to explode with worry. What would she do if he actually said the words she was dreading? *I think we should break up.*

The sand was dotted with brightly colored umbrellas and people stretched out on blankets to catch the rays. Near the water's edge, a little boy was building a sand castle, and farther down the beach an elderly lady was searching for shells.

Beau and Joni pulled off their shoes and waded knee-deep into the water. A few steps later, the tide pulled sand from under their feet as the surf rolled back into the sea.

Finally Beau took a deep breath and squinted at her in the bright sunlight. "So what was wrong with you last night? Were you trying to tell me you want to break up?"

Joni stopped and blinked at him in amazement, her mouth hanging open. "What?" she asked incredulously.

"You heard me," Beau said irritably. "I could tell

the minute you got in the car to go to the movie that something was bugging you. I tried to talk to you, and you weren't even listening. You were, like, a million miles away. It was the same when we got to the theater. You didn't say three words to me all night, and then you went to *sleep!*"

"I did not go to sleep!" Joni retorted. "How could I talk to you, anyway? You were busy flirting with Cami all night!"

Beau jerked his head around and gaped at her. He seemed genuinely shocked. "I wasn't flirting with Cami. She was just being friendly, that's all. That girl has changed so much. She's really a lot of fun now that she isn't super shy."

"She's changed, all right," Joni said grimly. "She's changed so much that she stole Todd away from Marissa just like that. And I'm supposed to think she's a lot of fun, too? Marissa's my friend, remember?" *Was,* she corrected herself silently.

"Well, I thought Cami was your friend, too," said Beau. "At least that's the impression I had."

"How can I stay friends with someone who would do a thing like that?" Joni demanded. "I mean, Marissa is really taking this whole breakup thing badly. She's hurting big-time. I'd help her get Todd back if I could."

Beau looked at her in alarm. "Butt out, Joni. It's

none of your business. How do you know it was definitely Cami who broke up Todd and Marissa, anyway? Did Marissa tell you that? Did you ever stop to think that maybe there was more to it than we know?"

Joni snorted in disgust. "Now you're taking Cami's side. Well, it's no wonder. She was hanging all over you *and* Todd last night. And believe me, I was really steamed."

"Come off it!" Beau said angrily. "It's *you* I like, not Cami. But what do you expect me to do when you acted like that last night? I told you, I was only talking to her. Get real."

Joni didn't answer right away. Beau had said the main thing she wanted to hear. He liked her. And she liked him as much as ever. If Cami came between them now, she knew it would be her fault, and she'd lose Beau forever. She couldn't let that happen.

"I'm sorry, Beau," Joni said finally. "I didn't mean to overreact. It's just that I've been really upset over Todd dumping Marissa. Then Cami got carried away with Todd and dumped Marissa, too. They've been best friends for ages. Imagine how Marissa must feel."

"Yeah, well, that is too bad," said Beau. "But I still think you should stay out of it. Let them handle their own lives."

"Oh, Beau, how can you say that?" Joni asked, shaking her head sadly. "Todd's your friend, too, isn't he?"

"Sure. So what?"

"What do you mean, so what?" Joni insisted. Suddenly a fabulous plan was beginning to form in her mind, a plan as great as anything Lindsey Jones had ever thought up. "You don't want to see Todd get used, do you?"

Beau shook his head and looked at her questioningly.

"Come on, let's head for the Snack Shack and get something to drink," Joni said, grabbing his hand. She knew a silly grin was spreading across her face, but she couldn't help it. "I think I know something we can do."

Chapter
Fifteen

It took a long time for Joni to convince Beau to go along with her idea.

"Don't you *see?*" she finally said in exasperation. "Cami took Todd away from Marissa. Now she's flirting with every guy in sight. She'll probably dump him as soon as somebody else comes along who's interesting."

"I find that a bit hard to believe," said Beau, shaking his head. "That's why I'm not going to do it."

"Are you a good enough friend to Todd to find out if I'm right?" Joni asked, shooting him a challenging look.

Beau scowled. "Give me a break, Joni! I hear what you're saying, but ..." He paused and looked out across the water, focusing on a pelican bobbing offshore. "I just don't know about this kind of stuff. It makes me really nervous."

"So?" Joni demanded. "Are you Todd's friend, Beau Maguire, or not?" She knew she couldn't let up now. "I *dare* you."

The look in his eyes told her she had won him over. *Guys can never resist a dare*, she thought triumphantly. *It works every time.*

When Joni approached her locker Monday morning, Marissa was already at hers. Joni noticed a tightness around the corners of Marissa's mouth as she worked the combination lock. Joni knew Marissa was only pretending that she hadn't seen her walk up.

"Hi, Marissa," Joni said. She held her breath, waiting for Marissa to respond. When she didn't, Joni tried again. "Listen, Marissa, I want you to know that I felt really bad about double-dating with Todd and Cami Friday night. I didn't want to, but Beau had already told them we would. Honest."

Marissa still didn't take her eyes off her lock. Shrugging, she said, "So? Who cares?"

Joni bit her lower lip and looked sadly at Marissa. She wanted to make her understand, but she knew Marissa's pride was probably hurt too badly to listen.

Joni fumbled for words. "I ... I just wanted you to know, that's all. I'm really sorry."

She hurriedly got out her books, closed her locker,

and headed up the hall, looking for Beau. She had to see if he was still going to go along with her scheme. Things weren't going too well so far.

Rounding a corner, she almost smacked into Crystal and Su-Su coming from the other direction.

"There you are. We were looking all over for you," said Crystal. She looked worried.

"Yeah, wait till we tell you what we just saw," Su-Su said somberly. "You're not going to like it."

"Really? What?" Joni asked, pretending to be surprised.

Su-Su let out a long breath and knitted her eyebrows together in a frown. "I hate to be the bearer of bad news, but Cami has Beau cornered in front of the gym. She's giving him her big-time flirting routine."

"And he seems to be enjoying it," added Crystal. "I'm really sorry, Joni."

"Yes!" shouted Joni, jamming her fist into the air.

"What?" Crystal and Su-Su asked in unison.

"Have you lost it?" asked Su-Su. "What are you talking about?"

Joni grinned. "It's working! Cami's falling for it! Beau's helping us play a trick on her. I mean, he doesn't actually know that but…"

"I don't get it," said Crystal. "What are you talking about?"

"Okay, this is what's happening," Joni began

patiently. "Number one, the only way Marissa is ever going to get Todd back is if he sees Cami for what she really is these days. Number two, Cami is so carried away with herself that she'll probably dump Todd if another cute guy acts really interested in her."

"You mean *Beau?*" Su-Su asked in astonishment. "Are you saying *you* put Beau up to flirting with her?"

"Well, I sort of tricked him," Joni said sheepishly. "I made him think he was doing Todd a big favor, and to cinch the deal—get this—I *dared* him to flirt with Cami."

"Are you sure you know what you're doing?" asked Crystal, sounding worried. "What if your little scheme backfires? What if he falls for her for real?"

"He won't," Joni assured her. "Trust me."

"Trust you?" Su-Su rolled her eyes. "I just hope *you* can trust *Beau.*"

Joni spotted Beau and Cami together in the halls three times that day. She wouldn't have admitted it even to Crystal or Su-Su, but she got a catch in her throat every single time she saw them.

Cami was pulling out all the stops, smiling at him and batting her eyes. Beau certainly didn't show any signs of being in pain, either. In fact Crystal had been right about one thing. Beau did seem to be eating it up. And hadn't he said not to count on much from him? So what was his idea of *much*, anyway?

Joni's self-confidence continued to plummet as she moped through one class after another. She avoided looking at Cami in science during third period, and didn't even care when her test paper came back marked with a C, the lowest grade she'd had in any subject all year.

I really hope I do know what I'm doing, Joni thought, *or my whole life is about to be over.*

Chapter Sixteen

No one mentioned Beau and Cami as the girls set up the answering machine for Boy Talk later that afternoon. Joni guessed that her friends weren't saying much because they had seen Beau and Cami together a lot during the day and didn't want to tell her about it. And Joni couldn't bear to bring up the subject herself because she didn't want her friends to see that her confidence in Beau was slipping.

It wasn't long before the Boy Talk phone began ringing.

Beep.

"I have a question, Boy Talk. If a guy asks you out, and you really want to go, how should you answer? Should you say yes, yeah, sure, I guess so, or what?

I've heard that it's not good to act *too* enthusiastic, even if you are. Call me No Response."

"Big deal," Joni grumbled when No Response hung up. "Some of the calls we get are just so trivial."

"It isn't trivial to *her*," Crystal pointed out. "She sounded as if it's really worrying her."

Joni sighed. She wished she weren't in such a rotten mood. And she knew her friends could see through her attitude. They had to know that she was worried about Beau, but they were just too polite to say so.

The telephone rang again.

Beep.

"Hi, Boy Talk. I got my science test back today, and I *aced* it!"

Good for you, Joni thought darkly, trying to forget her own less-than-wonderful grade.

"I've never had such a great score before," the caller went on. "I was really excited until I found out that my boyfriend barely passed. Now he's started teasing me and telling everybody that I'm some sort of big genius. What can I do? I guess you could call me Pain in the Brain."

Joni tuned out during the next couple of calls. She couldn't care less what kinds of problems those girls had. She had enough of her own. She went over to the window and stared out at nothing. What was

Beau doing at that very moment? Playing basketball with the guys? Or was he talking to Cami on the phone? And if he *was* on the phone with her, had she called him? Or had he called her?

The sick feeling in Joni's stomach was getting worse and worse. *How could I have been so stupid?* she wondered.

"Hey, Joni," Su-Su called, "come here and listen up. You're missing some good stuff."

Joni rejoined her friends at the desk just as the phone rang again.

Beep.

"Hi, Boy Talk. This is Cool One with a message for No Response. Listen, girlfriend, if you want to keep him asking you out, you'd better play it cool, like I do. Let him know you're a tiny bit interested, but don't get carried away. Play hard to get. Keep him thinking that he just might have some competition. Know what I mean?"

"Tell that to Cami," Joni said with a snort.

Crystal giggled and started to say something, but she was cut off by the phone.

Beep.

"Hey, Pain in the Brain, the exact same thing happened to me a couple of months ago. My boyfriend got really bent out of shape over my good grades. At first I thought it was my fault and that I should hide the fact that I'm smart. Then I figured out that it wasn't *me* he was mad at, at all. He was mad at himself for not trying harder. We started studying together, and now everything's great between us. Plus we're *both* getting good grades. Just call me Smartened Up."

A few more kids called in just to listen, but soon more advice started coming in.

Beep.

"Hi there, Boy Talk. I think Cool One was way off base with her advice to No Response. Think about the poor guy who's doing the asking. It may have taken him days to get up his nerve. He put his feelings on the line. If she doesn't act like she really wants to go, he may be sorry he asked her out in the first place. You can call me Sensitive."

"I agree with Sensitive," said Crystal, nodding. "I mean, boys have feelings, too, right?"

"You don't really think they worry about being turned down, do you?" scoffed Su-Su.

"Of course they do," said Crystal. "They're facing the big R word."

"Huh?" Joni said, puzzled.

"Rejection," Crystal said knowingly.

"Yeah, but ..." Su-Su hesitated. "Boys always act so confident and, you know, macho."

"It's just an act," Crystal assured her. "I found that out when Alison Hamel broke up with Evan. He asked *me* to help get them back together because he didn't have the guts to talk to her, remember?"

The phone rang again.

Beep.

"Hi, Boy Talk," said a familiar voice. "This is His Secret Love again."

Joni's mouth dropped open. *Cami!* She scrambled closer to the answering machine to hear every word.

"Have I got a problem for you," His Secret Love said with a giggle. "When I called before, I had a big crush on this one guy. Well, he broke up with his girlfriend, and we started going out. But now there's this other boy."

"She's talking about *Beau!*" Joni cried.

His Secret Love paused, and Joni almost exploded with anger.

"Anyway, this other boy has a girlfriend, too, but they're not getting along right now. I know. I saw them together Friday night—"

"What!" shrieked Joni.

"Shhh. Listen," warned Su-Su.

"—and you could tell they were mad. He's really, really cute, and I never dreamed he'd be interested in me. But he is! He's been flirting with me like crazy. Now I like *him*, too! What am I going to do?"

Joni felt her chin start to quiver as Cami hung up.

"What are *you* going to do?" she murmured. "What am *I* going to do?"

Chapter Seventeen

"We told you you were crazy for making Beau flirt with Cami," Su-Su said, shaking her head. "Didn't we say the whole plan might backfire? And it looks like it did."

"Don't say that, Su-Su," Crystal said. She put a sympathetic arm around Joni. "We don't know if Beau is really planning to cheat on you. Maybe he's just faking it with Cami."

"Thanks a lot, guys," Joni said in disgust. She moved away from Crystal, folding her arms across her chest. "You really know how to cheer a person up. And you know Cami wasn't calling in today to get advice for a problem. She was calling in to brag!"

"So what are you going to do about Beau?" asked Crystal.

Joni shrugged. "I don't have a clue. Maybe I can't do anything. I have this horrible feeling he's really fallen for Cami."

Joni was still depressed when she got home from Boy Talk. She couldn't take her eyes off the phone all evening, even while she was doing her homework. Why didn't it ring? Why didn't Beau call her and tell her something, anything, about what had happened with Cami? Joni couldn't believe he didn't realize that she'd want to know.

A couple of times she picked up the phone and started to punch in his number, but she kept losing her nerve. What if the worst really did come true and he told her he wanted to break up? And if she did call him and make a big deal out of his flirting with Cami, he'd probably remind her that it was her idea in the first place. How could she have been so stupid?

When Joni got to her locker the next morning, she was surprised to find Marissa waiting for her. Not only that, but Marissa was all smiles.

"Joni, guess what? Todd and I are back together!" she said, bouncing up and down with joy. "And guess what else? He said Cami broke up with him for another guy. I don't know who, but it doesn't matter because Todd said he was getting tired of the way Cami kept flirting with every guy in sight. He said he was thinking about breaking up with her, anyway.

And he really missed *me*! Isn't that terrific?"

Joni stared at her in amazement. "Cami broke up with Todd?" she blurted out. "But it was supposed to be the other way around. Todd was—" She clamped a hand over her mouth and stared at Marissa in horror.

"What do you mean, it was supposed to be the other way around?" Marissa asked, frowning. "What do you know about this, anyway?"

Joni gulped nervously. Now she had totally blown it. She'd have to think of an explanation fast, or she'd give away Boy Talk.

"Don't try to stall until you figure out how to worm out of this, Joni Sparkman," Marissa said angrily. "What did you have to do with Todd and me breaking up? You'd better tell me everything!"

"I ... I mean ..." Joni fumbled for words. "I know this doesn't look good, but it's not the way you think it is. Honest."

Marissa tapped her foot impatiently. "I'm waiting."

"Listen, Marissa, when you and Todd broke up, I felt really bad," Joni began. "I know you said you were the one who decided to break up and that you fixed Todd up with Cami, but deep down, I didn't believe that was what really happened. I had a feeling you still liked Todd and wanted him back. I don't know why I thought that. I just did."

Joni paused and took a deep breath. She had to

say this right, not just to protect Boy Talk, but also to save her friendship with Marissa.

"Anyway, when I saw what a flirt Cami had turned into, I decided I had to try to help you out," Joni went on. "What I can't understand is why she changed so much so quickly."

"I can explain that," Marissa said in a disgusted voice. "I had Todd fix her up for the Beach Bash with Marc Howe, but she was too shy to talk to him. I talked Todd into paying a lot of attention to her to help boost her self-confidence and make it easier for her to feel comfortable around boys. Wow! Was that ever a mistake! It helped her self-confidence, all right."

She sighed. "And did that girl ever have me fooled. I didn't realize she had a crush on Todd. I thought she just liked him as a friend. I should have figured it out, because she used every excuse she could think of for us to be a threesome so she could be around him. But that still doesn't explain what *you* had to do with all of this."

"I know this is hard to believe," Joni said in a rush, "but I thought if Todd saw Cami for what she really is, he'd break up with her and come back to you. And I wanted him to realize it fast, for your sake. So I got this brilliant idea to speed things up by having Beau flirt with her in front of Todd. I was hoping Todd would dump her, but I guess everything happened in reverse. Cami dumped Todd, and Beau must have fallen for Cami!"

"Oh, gosh, Joni. That's awful! You and I both made the same mistake, using our boyfriends to try and solve somebody else's problem," said Marissa. Shock was written all over her face.

Joni couldn't say a word. All she could do was choke back tears.

Marissa patted her sympathetically on the shoulders. "I know," she said hopefully. "I could have Todd talk to Beau."

Joni shook her head. "No," she managed to get out. "Thanks, but that might only make things worse."

She got the books for her morning classes and headed for Spanish class. So many tears were filling her eyes that everything seemed to be underwater. Her heart ached so much that she wasn't sure how she'd be able to get through a whole day of school. She had really blown things now.

Suddenly she heard someone calling her name.

"Joni! Hey, Joni, wait up. I need to talk to you."

It was Beau! She knew it without looking around. Her heart almost stopped. This was it: the moment she was dreading! He wanted to tell her that he liked Cami Petre instead of her!

She just couldn't face it right now. Without even a glance behind her, Joni took off running down the hall.

Chapter Eighteen

Joni managed to avoid Beau all morning. She took different routes between classes to keep from running into him. Once she saw him standing in the hall, checking in both directions as if he was looking for someone. Joni ducked into an empty classroom until he was gone. She even persuaded Su-Su and Crystal to eat lunch on the front steps of the school with her rather than going into the cafeteria at noon.

"I'm just not prepared to hear him say we're breaking up," she said around a bite of tuna salad sandwich. "I don't think I could stand it."

"I'll bet Cami must be feeling pretty proud of herself right now," grumbled Su-Su.

"Speaking of Cami, she wasn't in science class this

morning," said Joni, frowning. "She must be absent."

"Absent?" Crystal asked in surprise. "She didn't sound sick when she called Boy Talk yesterday afternoon."

"Who knows?" Joni shrugged. Cami's health was the least of her worries. On the other hand, maybe Cami would get very, very sick...

Suddenly a movement caught her attention in the corner of her eye. Looking around, she saw Beau coming out the door nearest the cafeteria and heading her way.

"Oh, no," she said under her breath. "Oh, guys, help! This could be it. I'm dead!"

"It looks like you're going to have to face him now whether you want to or not," said Crystal. "Come on, Su-Su. Let's give the two of them some privacy." She gave Joni's shoulder a squeeze and whispered, "Good luck."

Su-Su and Crystal picked up what was left of their lunches and went inside, leaving Joni alone on the steps. Beau was heading straight toward her, and her heart pounded in time with his footsteps.

"Hi, Joni," he said in a somber voice as he sat down next to her. "Please don't run away. I really need to talk to you."

"Okay," she said softly, but sitting there was the hardest thing she'd ever had to do. Her pulse was throbbing in her temples, and her emotions were building up like a volcano about to erupt. Suddenly she couldn't hold back any longer. Before Beau could say anything else, she blurted out, "You're going to break up with me, aren't you? Cami dumped Todd because she has *you* now! That's what you're going to say, isn't it?"

Beau looked her straight in the eye and didn't answer. The look on his face told her Joni had blown it one more time.

"Is that what you really think?" he said between clenched teeth. "*You're* the one who put me up to flirting with the girl, you know. *You're* the one who said I should help out my old buddy Todd. Well, I flirted with her, and she dumped him. I did everything you wanted me to, and now you think I cheated on you."

Joni's heart was in her throat as Beau stood up and started down the steps.

"For your information"—he paused and looked back over his shoulder at her—"what I wanted to tell you was that she called me last night after she broke up with Todd. I told her that *you're* the girl I like, the *only* one. But I guess we're history now because you don't trust me."

Joni was speechless. She stared at Beau in open-mouthed horror as he scuffed across the school grounds, his head down, his fists stuffed into his jeans pockets.

She jumped to her feet. "Beau!" she called out. Racing down the steps, she hurried after him. "Beau, I'm sorry," she began as she caught up with him. "You don't know how sorry I am."

He kept on walking and didn't look up.

"I was just so scared that I completely lost it," she said. "And Cami's so cute and all and…" She looked around helplessly, searching for the right words. But she couldn't think of anything to say that would make things right again. And Beau wouldn't even look at her now.

Joni stopped and sighed. "I guess you don't like me anymore, do you?"

Beau slowed to a stop, too, and looked at her for a few moments without speaking. Then he shrugged. "That's not true. But you can be pretty frustrating sometimes, Joni. Can't you just chill once in a while?"

Joni swallowed hard. "I'll try," she promised around the huge lump of joy forming in her throat. She hadn't lost him after all! Not yet, anyway.

"Just get a grip on yourself, okay?" Beau said, sighing and taking her hand. "You have to trust me. I really want you to be my girlfriend, Joni."

All she could do was nod. She knew that if she tried to speak, she would burst into tears. And she *would* get a grip on herself. She would keep her emotions in control if it killed her. Beau was too special to ever let him get away.

Chapter Nineteen

Joni was still walking on air when she got to Crystal's house for Boy Talk after school.

"Beau and I are going to the movies again on Friday night," she said excitedly. She was babbling uncontrollably, but she didn't care. She knew her friends understood how happy she was. "He's going to talk to Todd and see if he and Marissa want to double with us. Aren't you glad Todd and Marissa are back together? I sure am. Anyway, I told Beau I'd talk to you guys about the four of you coming along, too."

"Chris hasn't asked me out yet, but I'm pretty sure he'll want to go," said Su-Su.

"Evan, too," said Crystal, her dimple appearing as she gave Joni a big smile. "And yeah, I'm really glad Marissa and Todd are back together. At least she isn't *double*-dumped anymore, right?"

Su-Su grinned. "The only one who's dumped now is Cami!"

At 3:31 the Boy Talk phone began ringing.

Beep.

"Listen, Boy Talk, I've got a very important question. How do boys like girls to kiss? I need to know— *immediately!* You can call me ... gosh, I don't know. I guess you can just call me Help!"

Joni, Crystal, and Su-Su were all laughing when Help! hung up.

"She sounds desperate," said Su-Su, shaking her head.

"She must have a date tonight," Joni added.

Crystal's face lit up. "Maybe we should give her some advice," she said. "After all, we've all been kissed, right? We're practically experts."

"We could tell her not to hold her breath, because if it's a long kiss she could explode," suggested Su-Su. She blew out her cheeks and made a popping sound as she let out her breath.

"Or we could tell her not to put on too much lip gloss or she could slide right off his face," said Joni, giggling at the idea.

"Come on, guys. Get serious," said Crystal. "She asked for real advice."

"If you ask me, those things were pretty real," Su-Su said.

Crystal threw her a disgusted look. "Well, I'm going to think up some different advice, something that will really help her out."

Just as Crystal picked up a pencil and pad and began scribbling, the phone rang again.

Beep.

There was a long pause. Finally a familiar voice said, "Hi, Boy Talk. This is His Secret Love again. I know you're probably getting tired of me calling in, but I have a humongous problem this time."

"It's Cami," said Joni in amazement. "Doesn't that girl ever give up?"

On the other end of the line, Joni could hear Cami crying softly. "I've done something really awful, and I don't know what to do about it. I couldn't even go to school today. I couldn't face anybody, especially the girl who used to be my best friend."

Cami sniffed back tears and went on. "You see, it all started when her boyfriend started paying a lot of attention to me. Boys don't usually do that, and I was really flattered. And he's so cute and so friendly that I couldn't help having a crush on him, even though I knew he belonged to her. The more he flirted with me, the bigger my crush got until I couldn't think about anything else. I worked up my nerve and started flirting back. That's when things started getting out of hand, and I really went after him. I didn't even care what my best friend thought."

She paused, blowing her nose loudly. "Then he broke up with her and started going with me. I was so happy. As long as I had him, I thought I didn't need her anymore, so I sort of dumped her, too. But flirting was so much fun—it was like I had just discovered it after being shy all my life. Anyway, I started paying attention to lots of guys. It was fun when they flirted back. That's when I got a second crush on a boy who also had a girlfriend who was a friend of mine."

She paused, and Joni folded her arms.

"That's Beau she's talking about now," she said.

"Shhh," cautioned Su-Su.

"At first I liked both of them, but I started liking the second boy more, so I broke up with the first boy. I thought the second boy really liked me, but then he told me he likes his girlfriend and not me. I don't have a boyfriend anymore, and my former best friend *hates* me. I realize now all I did was make a big fool of myself."

Cami paused again and then said in a teary voice, "I want my best friend to know how sorry I am, and that I want her friendship back, but I don't know what to do."

Nobody said a word for a moment after Cami hung up.

"Wow," Joni finally said. "I think she really feels guilty about what she did."

"Yeah," said Crystal. "That sort of changes things."

"What do you mean?" asked Su-Su. "How could that change anything?"

"Well, if she really did learn something from all this—like you have to leave your friends' boyfriends alone no matter what—then maybe Marissa could forgive her," said Crystal.

"Do you think we could get them together so they could talk about it?" Joni asked excitedly. "It might be a start."

"Yeah," said Su-Su. "Maybe we could call both of them and invite them to meet us somewhere and not tell them that the other one was going to be there."

"Sneaky," said Crystal, shaking a finger at Su-Su and grinning. "But I love it!"

Behind them, the Boy Talk phone rang and rang, but the three girls were too busy making plans to listen.

"They could come to my house," offered Su-Su. Then she frowned and added, "Unless, of course, Patrick's home. He's the world's biggest snoop. He might hear what they say and spread it around."

"If I can get rid of Hannah, they can come to my house," Joni said.

"Maybe we should think of a place where they can

— 102 —

really be alone," said Crystal. "They might not talk honestly in front of us."

The girls lapsed into thought. A moment later the phone rang.

Beep.

"Hi, Boy Talk. This is Double Dumped."

Joni gasped and sprang to attention. "It's Marissa!" she cried.

Crystal and Su-Su were listening, too.

"I just heard His Secret Love's message, and if she's who I think she is and she's really sorry, we should talk. I'm not sure things can ever be the same, but I've really missed her, and maybe we can at least start to be friends again."

"Yay! Yay!" the girls shouted in unison when Double Dumped hung up. They jumped up and down and hugged each other for at least five minutes.

"Boy Talk really worked this time," said Su-Su when they finally settled down.

"It certainly did," said Crystal. "And do you know the best part? I think Marissa and Cami both learned something important from all this."

Joni nodded and closed her eyes. She couldn't forget about her own foolish mistakes and about how she had almost lost Beau. "They aren't the only ones," she said and smiled happily to herself.

Hi, guys! Su-Su here. Hope you liked Double Dumped. *Here's a sneak peek at Book #5:* Tongue-Tied:

"Hi, Boy Talk. This is a message for Tongue-Tied," Su-Su said. "I know how hard it is sometimes to be cool around the guy you like. Believe me, I've been there. But there's one thing you have to remember. Breaking the ice is the first step to melting his heart.

"Just look him straight in the eye, smile, and say hello. Trust me. It's easy and—"

"Su-Su! Hang up! Right now!"

It was Crystal, trying to get her attention. Su-Su frowned at her friend, who was looking at her in horror.

Putting her hand over the mouthpiece, Su-Su told her, "I'll be off in a minute."

"Sorry, Tongue-Tied," she said into the receiver. "Anyway, what I wanted to say is, it really works. Try it, and then call in again, and I'll tell you what to do next." She started to hang up and then remembered something important. "Just call me Ice Breaker," she said happily.

When she hung up, Joni and Crystal were both standing there staring at her. Their faces were storm clouds.

"Do you realize what you just did?" Joni demanded.

BETSY HAYNES wrote her first book when she was nine years old. It was about a frog named Peppy who leaves his lily pad to see the world. Today most of her books are based on things that happened to her and her friends when they were in middle school and junior high—Betsy says she's forever thirteen!

Betsy lives on Marco Island, Florida. She and her husband, Jim, have two grown children, two dogs, and a black cat with extra toes. She enjoys traveling and spending time on her boat, *Nut & Honey*. And she really loves to talk on the phone!

WRITE TO "DEAR BOY TALK"

NEED ADVICE ABOUT

DATING?   **FRIENDSHIP?**   **ROMANCE?**

Joni, Crystal, and Su-Su may have an answer for you!

Just write to *Dear Boy Talk* at this address:

Random House, Inc.
201 East 50th Street
New York, NY 10022

Attn: "Dear Boy Talk"
28th Floor

Let us know what's on your mind. From secret crushes to broken hearts to major embarrassments, Boy Talk™ can help! We can't publish every letter, but we can promise to print a select few in the back of every new Boy Talk book.

Too shy to share your romance problems? Boy Talk fans can give advice for readers' problems, too! Letters began appearing in Boy Talk #2: DUDE IN DISTRESS. Just pick a problem and write to the above address—and you just might see *your* letter in print!

Dear Boy Talk:
My best friend has a crush on the same boy I do. She says if I go out with him, she'll stop being my best friend! I want to go out with this boy, but I want to stay friends with my best friend. I need advice.

Totally Confused
Virginia

Dear Confused:
Boyfriends come and go, but best friends can last a lifetime. Maybe the two of you should sit down and talk this situation over and decide where your loyalties are.

Crystal

Dear Confused:
What I want to know is, who does <u>he</u> have a crush on? You or your friend? Or neither one of you? It would be a shame to wreck your friendship over somebody who couldn't care less!

Joni

Dear Confused:
Sometimes a boy you've hardly paid attention to suddenly looks good as soon as somebody else gets a crush on him. You start seeing all sorts of cool things about him that you've never noticed before. That's normal. Just don't get carried away with your crush until you get to know him better and find out if he's worth the hassle of losing your best friend.

Su-Su

Dear Boy Talk:
There is this guy I've been dating for over one and a half months, and we broke up once, but got back together. The problem is, most of his friends are girls. Every time we want to do something, one of them tags along. I feel like he doesn't want to be alone with me. What should I do?

Lost in Love
Connecticut

Dear Lost:
**It sounds to me as if he's not ready for
romance yet. If he sees all girls as
"friends," maybe that's how he sees you,
too. You could be wasting your time.**

Joni

Dear Lost:
Have you ever thought about inviting another
boy to go along on your dates? Then he'd get
the point pretty fast. Maybe his "girl" friend
and your "boy" friend would hit it off, and you
and your boyfriend could be alone at last!

Su-Su

Dear Lost:
I hope Su-Su was only joking. I feel
sorry for your boyfriend. Maybe he's
nervous about being alone with you.
Guys worry about rejection. Maybe
he thinks if you get to know him better, you won't like him. Try dropping
some hints that you think he's really
special.

Crystal

Dear Boy Talk:
There is a boy who I think is cute, nice, and funny, but he's also going out with my best friend! I really like him. Help!

Single
Virginia

Dear Single:
Your letter sounds a lot like Totally Confused from Virginia's. In fact, you're both from the same state. Excuse me for thinking like a detective, but are you two best friends and talking about the same guy? I'm going to dig the envelopes from your letters out of the trash and see if they're from the same town. In the meantime, you two had better talk!

Joni

Dear Single:
It doesn't take a detective to figure out that lots of girls have your problem. There are only so many cute, nice, funny guys in the world, right? And definitely not enough to go around! But is he the only one in your grade? Your whole school? Just think, if you could find yourself another cute, nice, funny guy, you and your best friend could double-date!

Su-Su

Dear Single:
I think your problem is a little more complicated than that. It's nice that you're being so sensitive to your friend's feelings by not barging in and trying to steal him away from her. If you can get his attention and be nice to him without actually flirting, then maybe if he and your girlfriend ever break up, he'll want to date you.

Crystal

Dear Boy Talk:
I'm the smartest kid in my class, but most of my friends treat me as if I were a baby—even my best friend! I don't like being treated like this, but how can I let my friends know without hurting their feelings?

Not a Baby
North Carolina

Dear Not:
I sort of know how you feel. I'm the smallest person in my class, and sometimes people treat me like I'm still in diapers. The time it bothered me the most was when the boy I like treated me like his kid sister. I just kept reminding myself that I was a lot more grown-up than he thought, and pretty soon he saw it for himself. He's my boyfriend now!

Crystal

Dear Not:
Does being so smart embarrass you? Have you ever thought that you might be putting yourself down to hide how brainy you are and not know you're doing it? You might be trying so hard to act like one of the gang that your friends are all getting the wrong impression.

Dear Not:
It's awful being misunderstood. It happens to me sometimes, too. Some people think that just because I like to be a little dramatic sometimes, I'm a zany bubblehead. My best friends know better, because I can talk to them about my feelings. Maybe you're keeping too much inside. Try opening up more to your friends. If they really are your friends, they'll understand.

Su-Su

Dear Boy Talk:
There's this guy at school who is really cute, nice, and smart. The only problem is, I don't know if he even thinks of me as a friend. We are the exact opposite of one another, so even if we were friends, I don't think we'd understand one another. What should I do?

Opposite Crazy
Michigan

Dear Opposite:
Opposites really do attract, you know. We get bored with ourselves sometimes, and can easily fall for someone who's mysterious and exciting. I say go for it! You could have lots of fun learning to understand each other.

Su-Su

Dear Opposite:
I can't imagine having a relationship with someone I had nothing in common with. Talk about boring! Part of the fun of having a boyfriend is

doing things together that you both enjoy and sharing moments that are special to both of you. I'd be careful about getting involved with a guy who's so different from you.

Crystal

Dear Opposite:
I think Su-Su and Crystal are both missing the issue here. How can you decide if he's the boy for you until you get to know him better? Maybe he's not so different after all. Or maybe he *is* too different. You'd be better off making friends with him and finding out.

Joni

Dear Boy Talk:
A couple of guys like me. I like them, too, but they are so immature. Why are boys so immature? Why do they have to turn everything into a contest? Should I go out with any of them?

Miss Mature
Tennessee

Dear Mature:
Boy, am I an expert on that subject! My boyfriend Beau is the most immature boy in the world. Let's face it, though. Boys are much slower than girls. Go ahead and go out with one of them if you like him enough to put up with the way he acts. But if you don't, forget it. Wait for them to grow up!

Joni

Dear Mature:
Check their star signs. I'm serious. If you want a mature boyfriend, date only boys born under Scorpio, Virgo, or Capricorn. They are serious, sensitive, and reliable. Avoid Sagittarius, Gemini, and Aries—unless you want someone who's fun-loving and a little crazy. (I ought to know, I'm a Gemini!)

Su-Su

Dear Mature:
I think boys act immature sometimes because they're trying to show off for us girls. The trouble is, they don't know how dumb they look. Just be patient, and remember, you don't have to play their silly games.

Crystal

Dear Boy Talk:
I told my friends I was grounded the other day, but I was really out on a date with the hottest boy in fifth grade! I think one of my friends is also going out with him, too, though. Now I'm afraid she'll find out I <u>wasn't</u> grounded and that I was really on a date with her boyfriend. Should I break up with him or with her?

I'm Trapped
Ohio

Dear Trapped:
Whoa! Why all the secrecy? Why did you tell your friends you were grounded? Do you know for sure that your friend is going out with this boy? Did he want you to not tell anybody about your date? I think you need to get some answers before you make any big decisions.

Joni

Dear Trapped:
Just because this boy is the hottest boy in fifth grade doesn't mean he's the right one for you. It just means he's popular. It also sounds as if you're really concerned about what your friend thinks of you. If I were you, I'd go slow and make sure I didn't lose the wrong person.

Crystal

Dear Trapped:
He may be hot, but is he cool? What kind of guy would date one girl and then go out with her friend behind her back? If that's what he's doing, you'd be better off without him. You'd even be better off <u>grounded</u>.

Su-Su

Dear Boy Talk:
My ex-boyfriend just dumped me. I think he knows I still like him and want to get back together with him. We used to do everything together. Now he's calling me names, and I'm thinking maybe I did something wrong.

Helpmeplease
Georgia

Dear Helpmeplease:
Don't blame yourself. If you did something so bad that it would make him call you names, you'd know it! On the other hand, maybe you're chasing him too

much, and he's using name-calling to get you to back off. Either way, he sounds like a jerk. Be glad you're rid of him.

Joni

Dear Helpmeplease:
Maybe he likes someone else. Face it. It happens. And guys aren't always the greatest at breaking up gently. No matter what the reason, if he's calling you names, you definitely don't need him. I know it hurts to lose him, but start looking around for someone new.

Crystal

Dear Helpmeplease:
Whatever you do, don't let him know he's bugging you! And definitely don't sink to his level and call him names back. Be an actress. Hold

your head up high and smile. Show everybody
that you don't deserve all those nasty names.
Then they'll see that <u>he's</u> the one with the
problem, not you!

Su-Su

Dear Boy Talk:
My two best friends don't like one another. I just
met one of them and I've known the other one
since kindergarten! I don't want to lose either of
them. What should I do?

Clueless
Louisiana

Dear Clueless:
Don't let yourself get trapped in the
middle. Talk to each one and tell her
why you think she's special. Then go
on to tell her what's so special about
your <u>other</u> friend. Try to make them
both understand that you see them

as individuals and that they aren't in competition for your friendship.

Crystal

Dear Clueless:
Jealousy can really tear you down. Maybe they're jealous of each other because they don't know each other that well. Try to convince them to communicate with each other. Don't forget, communication is the key to solving problems. They might even find that since they have enough in common with you to be your friend, they have things in common with each other.

Joni

Dear Clueless:
It must be nice to be so popular that you have girls fighting to be your friend. (Just kidding. It sounds awful.) Since you're in the middle

whether you want to be or not, try asking them to give each other a chance for your sake.

Su-Su

Dear Boy Talk:
I really don't know what to do with my boyfriend. He never pays attention to me when we're at school with his friends. But when I talk to him on the phone, he's an angel. Should I break up with him?

Yes or No
Pennsylvania

Dear Yes or No:
Tell me about it! Beau used to drive me crazy doing the very same thing. I finally found out that peer pressure makes boys do that. They don't want the other guys to call them wimps because they have girlfriends. It's true. Boys who haven't started dating hang together a

lot and tease the guys who do. It's pretty weird. If you can't stand the hassle, call it quits.

Joni

Dear Yes or No:
I think he's showing you his true feelings on the phone. But, as Joni says, he doesn't want to make a fool of himself in front of his friends. If you're sweet and understanding, he'll eventually come around.

Crystal

Dear Yes or No:
It's a real putdown when a guy acts as if you don't exist in front of his friends. It's another sign of immaturity. If you ask me, this guy needs a baby-sitter, not a girlfriend!

Su-Su

<u>Disaster of the Day</u>

Dear Boy Talk:
My boyfriend's best friend really hates me. He's always making fun of me when the three of us hang out, and I've heard he says mean stuff about me behind my back, too. I'm afraid he might try to convince my boyfriend to break up with me! What should I do?

Bud Repellent
Arizona

Remember Bud Repellent's letter?
Here's some advice from all you Boy Talk readers:

Dear Bud Repellent:
You've got a serious problem here. Your boyfriend's friend is a total jerk. He has no right to convince your boyfriend to dump you, so don't worry about that. Talk to your boyfriend and tell him all the bad things his friend did to you. Ask him what his friend has against you. If your boyfriend listens to his friend about dumping you, then your boyfriend is a big jerk, too.

Welcome to Help
New York

Dear Bud Repellent:
Tell your boyfriend how you feel. Maybe he can talk to
his friend and tell him about all your good points. If
that doesn't work, talk to one of your girlfriends and
see if she wants to go out with your boyfriend's friend.
Maybe they'll go out and hit it off, and she'll tell him
what a great person you are.

Helping You
New Jersey

Dear Bud Repellent:
I would tell your boyfriend how you felt about the situation, or talk to his best friend and ask him what's so
wrong with you. If he still teases you, tell him to bug
off! I wouldn't worry about him telling your boyfriend. If
your boyfriend really liked you, then he won't break up
with you over what his best friend said!

Not Really a Know-It-All
North Carolina

Disaster of the Day

Dear Boy Talk:
I've been dating this guy for about six months. He's the type of guy who likes to go places, and I don't have a problem if he wants to go alone or with friends. But when I want to go somewhere, he either wants to go too or he tells me I shouldn't go. How can I solve this problem?

Get Up & Go!
Florida

Joni   Su-su   Crystal

Write in soon, BoyTalk readers!
Get Up & Go needs some serious help!

PLAY

EVERYONE'S-A-WINNER GAME!

Grand Prize: An AT&T Phone
Additional Prizes: A Boy Talk Phone Card
                          A Boy Talk Key Chain

Details on how to claim your prize can be found on the back of your game piece insert. If the game piece is missing from your book, you can write to:

Boy Talk Game Piece
201 East 50th Street
MD 30-2
New York, NY 10022

Just send us your name and address and we'll mail you a free replacement game piece. Hurry—*offer good only while supplies last!*